MW00513848

THE SCHOOL

The School

Carl L. Trombley

Eloquent Books
New York, New York

Eloquent Books
An imprint of AEG Publishing Group
845 Third Avenue, 6th Floor—6016
New York, NY 10022
http://www.eloquentbooks.com

ISBN-13: 978-1-60860-147-9
ISBN-10: 1-60860-147-1

Book Designer: Bruce Salender

Printed in the United States of America

Acknowledgements

While golfing one morning, my playing partner suggested that I write a book about schools. I had just three putted for a double bogie and figured that he just wanted me to get involved in the writing process to keep me away from the golf course. We eventually won the match, but he had planted a thought that I couldn't resist.

During my career I spent many years as an elementary school principal. After a few years doing grants and curriculum in the central office, I had the opportunity to be an acting high school principal. Upon retiring, I entered the consulting business that took me around the area and state.

Much of the consulting work involved writing educational specifications for school building projects. The process of developing the specs meant spending time visiting and interviewing principals and staffs, walking hallways, visiting classrooms and observing the flow of students within the buildings.

The thoughts and situations written in the text of *The School* are based upon my experiences as well as my visitations to others schools and comments made by the principals in over ten different high schools in the state. Obviously, some situations are my imagination. Humor is a good thing and I have always enjoyed laughing at some of the drama over which I, and others, had no control. It sure beats wringing of one's hands and whining!

As I wrote I gave each page to my wife, Ann. A reading teacher herself, she has infinite wisdom as to what is readable and what is insane. Further, she knows me better than I know myself. That can be scary at times, but I rely on her judgment in all matters. I am a wise man.

As my wife of over 44 years read the pages, she would give me instant feedback. Without her input I might have stopped and moved onto other writing thoughts that are in the back of my mind. That I finished this book is on her. It was a joy for me to hear her chuckle and give her frequent response of "Cute." My thanks to her is enormous. Her monitoring of my writing and overall behavior is totally appreciated.

As I developed the story, I gave it to my son-in-law, David Clough. The Big Guy, my tag for him, read what I had given him and urged me to continue. I needed input from a man because much of the story involves "guy" situations. I also didn't want to include too much educational jargon, thinking it might hinder the story line. My thanks are extended to David for reading the text and responding in a positive manner. He is a good man and a perceptive reader of good material, at least in my mind.

Another friend from Gig Harbor, Washington, gave me valuable feedback on what I had written. Linda Stackpole is a fluent reader and a bright lady. Her comments and input were welcome and I thank her for the time she invested in reading what had been developed at the time of her perusal. Her husband, Tom, awaits the final draft.

My daughters, Carla, Jennifer, and Kristi reacted to sections of the text as they either read portions or I read it to them. I have always enjoyed their laughter and they didn't disappoint me in their responses. One of the best things about being a father is to hear your children laugh! I treasure them and their senses of humor. Genetically, they got my DNA for funny situations. Good on them!

As to my golfing partner, Joe Przybyloski, I must give him thanks for the suggestion of the project as well as his hospitality and concession of occasional putts. His kind and thoughtful wife, Lucy, has been gracious enough to read most of what I have written and her feedback has been huge in motivating me to continue to write.

A former colleague, Tony Spino, took time to read the initial draft and gave some valuable suggestions regarding the text. My thanks to him for the time he invested on my behalf.

I would be remiss not to mention the thousands of school people, both students and professionals, for lending their memories for my use. Perhaps they may find some of their experiences as they read *The School*.

Introduction

Each of us has an alma mater, a school from which we graduated or attended. No one leaves without a preponderance of good thoughts. Those high school days for most were the last of being a free spirit. Though we might have had a part-time job, our parents or guardians footed the bill for our expenses. Those days were among the best days of our lives.

A high school is more than an institution for learning. It had been a safe haven until Columbine-like tragedies made their way into them. While it might be a safer place now with more advanced security, some of the freedoms we older people enjoyed are not available to this and forthcoming generations.

For this generation and those that come, they may have stories we never experienced. They may involve such things as police or lockdowns. Whatever their stories evolve into memories, they will connect them to Their School.

Memorial High School, The School, is not unlike any other high school. A dedicated, knowledgeable, and hard working principal is at the helm. The staff is diligent and focused on student learning. The School is made up of good professional people as are most high schools everywhere.

Though at times, The School may seem dysfunctional, it is not. Personnel bring perceived or real problems which the principal attempts to deflect or solve. Brain Witaker, the principal, does and makes a concentrated effort to assist rather than blame. He is a good leader, acting with empathy and discretion.

Every school has its teaching and staff characters. Their faults or idiosyncrasies are seen by the students and become fodder for nicknames. For the most part, the nicknames are done in a harmless way. For example, one such teacher was "tagged" in my school. She was one of everyone's favorite teachers. She was a caring and creative teacher but right now I can't recall her real name, just her nickname.

It is important to understand that schools do no exist in isolation. Outside factors such as Boards of Education policies or changes in policies force the people inside of the schools to adjust. Pressure groups of one form or another also impact on those within a school. Most often these groups have a political base of some sort. Individuals in The School must deal with the problems the outside forces create and face the reality that the building is not theirs. It belongs to the community and they are employees, temporary entities in a broader, bigger picture.

In this story the outside factors from a local tavern, a football fundraising group, and a change in a Board policy create problems for the principal and some staff members. Though depicted in humorous terms, these situations may be similar to some a building principal may encounter in a large high school.

Not many student names can be found in the story. Students, to me and other professionals, are not subjects of humor. Students are the sunshine that brightens the classrooms and hallways. Students are the reason that schools are alive with laughter and noise as they turn their experiences into memories. They are the reason schools exist.

May you remember your school in endearing terms as you read about the one year in the life of the principal of Memorial High School, the people within it, the situations that arise, and as all strive to work in the best interests of the students and The School.

Chapter One

As he pulled open the main front door of the building he was met with a rush of stale air created by the vacuum of the entry way. The faint odor of pot wafted past his nostrils as his mind recalled that the head custodian, Billy Evans, "toked" while cleaning that area; well, every area to be exact.

Brian Witaker, the 45 year old principal of Memorial High School, noticed the sexual related graffiti on the "Home of the Beavers" sign over the entry way into the main lobby. It was too high for him to reach to attempt to wipe it clean so he calculated that it was either the work of someone on a ladder, or one of the taller boys in the school. Most likely it was Evans. School was not scheduled to begin the new year for two more days.

Witaker was a Navy veteran and had attended college upon his discharge from the service. Of average height and build, he had an honest face and maintained his person well. His military background showed in his short haircuts, well-shined shoes, and respectful behavior. His common sense approach to education and true interest in the welfare of the students found him rapidly promoted. He was proud that he could remain calm in situations which triggered anger in most people.

According to the most aggressive students he was a "cool dude." His first year of being the top school administrator was one of observing and creating a level of trust with the faculty, staff, and most of the students. To most, he was a good guy in the right position. He owed much of his success to his wife and family. His son and daughter, both in elementary school, had adjusted well to the move into their new school upon his appointment to his position. His wife supported him in everything that he did or attempted to do. While he was able to put his full concentration into his daily tasks, they were never far from his mind. His professional and personal lives were one but separate and he had learned to move from one to the other, leaving each behind as he moved to the other.

He opened his office door, threw his jacket on a chair, started his computer, and began his day. He downloaded the list of all faculty and staff and thought about each as he did so. He placed a yellow pad and pencil next to him for notations.

Of a total of 200 personnel, he noted that there were many with "problems" that he had to consider. Three were of questionable sexual preference, four had either alcohol or drug problems, two were inclined to be too playful with one another in the faculty lounge or the custodial closet, one was a "peeker" who may have drilled a hole from the English office into the girls lavatory, six were untenured but gave evidence that they could perform well enough to stay, and four new teachers were on the list. Several other idiosyncrasies had surfaced during his first year, none of major concern to him at this point It was a good group with the flaws found in any faculty of that size. His job was to make them better.

The faculty was about half male and half female. More males were found in the math and science departments while English and the Arts were predominately female.

Department chair positions were selected by a combined teacher/administration panel, and they had chosen well. The only contention surfaced when Mrs. Fielder was picked as chair of the math department. While she certainly had all the qualifications, she tended to pad her own schedule with AP and honors courses leaving the more difficult classes to others. Thus she became known as the Prime Number, divisible only by herself.

Witaker had made many friends in the English department when he changed the girl's lavatory located in the department area into a female staff lavatory. He had the peek hole repaired, glass mirrors installed to replace the metallic ones, and had replaced the older toilet seats with new ones. The custodial staff painted a mauve oil base over any graffiti and a new ceiling fan gave better air circulation in the room. Each stall was keyed so that each teacher had her own assigned stall, this way they could comfortably sit rather that "hover." A part-time matron was employed to maintain the lavatory forcing the full-time matron to the second floor girl's lavatory.

The English staff responded by having students do less diagramming of sentences and more reading. A win-win situation had evolved by the simple move of lavatories. Several pregnant English teachers were particularly happy and one even named her new son after him. The men didn't complain, they just continued to use the deep sink in the custodial closet.

As with most faculties, the range of teaching abilities flowed from excellent to average. He had been fortunate in getting two teacher resignations of less than satisfactory teachers in his first year. The two simply got tired of his sitting in their classrooms and the follow-up conferences. They referred to him as Sitting Bill or the Yellow Pad. He had addressed their resignation letters to the superintendent replacing his name with Sitting Bill on The School letterhead.

Teaching abilities related to teacher performance was one of his areas of focus for the coming year. As with some of their students, teachers did not always perform up to their abilities. It isn't easy to do it day after day, both in-school and outside factors affected daily performance. He made a notation to diminish as many in-school distractions as possible.

He was concerned that many of the teachers talked to their subjects and not to the students. Secondary school teachers tended to do that and he planned to do two workshops on teaching techniques, both scheduled for tomorrow, a staff development day for teachers. The focus of the workshops would be Teaching Techniques. In the first, he would teach exactly as most of the teachers did in their classrooms. In the second he would model the content of the first. He made a note to do several follow-up observations in the classrooms of those who were the worst offenders during the month of October.

The Art department was solid with one exception. Mrs. Thiesman continued to want to have the students paint nudes in her advanced drawing class. To the consternation of the rest of the art teachers, her class was filled with boys, none of whom had any interest or talent in art. The legend of her having a professional nude model pose several years ago led to the increased enrollment. Not knowing of the reason for the heavy enrollment of males, the last accreditation team gave high praise for the number of males interested in the arts, a rarity in most high schools.

The three music teachers were excellent. The band had won several awards in competitions and the director creatively utilized all the members during the football games by forming a block letter BEAVS during halftime. His goal was to have enough members to complete the word. The choral director made the most of the talent she had been given. However, she had made the mistake of consulting the Foreign Language department to assist in doing Christmas music throughout the world at the annual Winter Festival. It wasn't until after the performance that she discovered that two of the Hispanic songs contained profanities. Mr. Sanchez denied any wrong doing on behalf of his department but was seen laughing hysterically during the performance. Witaker noted that he would have to monitor the music selections with the choral teacher.

The third teacher was untenured but had done a good job with the general music elective and the course showed an increase in selection for the coming school year. He made a note to talk to the young man about his attire, especially the tight trousers and his hip thrusting during his guitar renditions of the Beatles.

The Social Studies department was as average as one could be. No outstanding scholars roamed their classrooms. The electives included a study of the local government and it became a controversial subject each election year as politicians came to sell their platforms and handout free pencils. Over the years they relied heavily on the straw poll conducted in the class as an indicator of how parents would vote at election time. They were totally confused by last year's poll when candidate Bruce Johnson won by a large margin as the students simply put BJ as their choice for mayor. He knew it would be a better year in the local government class because it was a non election year.

Psychology was a very popular selection in the department, particularly with the Goths, skinheads, and spiked hair students. He made a note to have each security officer attend the course.

The PE department had an excellent female staff and a very average male staff. Traditionally, they also taught Health and the women did an outstanding job. The male staff had less success in explaining the reproductive system, one even referring to an orgasm as an organism and an ejaculation as an evacuation. They male staff had sent a memo at the end of the year expressing their concern about the growing fungus problem in the boy's locker room. To address the increase in athlete's feet and jock itch was their only recommendation for improvement for their department.

Witaker had the most grief from the Business Department. Their new computer lab had been incorrectly installed and he had spent the first month getting it corrected. Because they had to use chalk or white boards during the interim, there were frequent absences. He made a note to have all the computers checked prior to the opening of school so that his No Business department would improve their attendance.

The Foreign Language group confused him. The two ladies who taught French were aloof in their contacts with fellow teachers. Alberto Sanchez, the head of the department, often mumbled Hispanic vulgarities during staff meetings. The one Latin teacher who had attended a Jesuit college was prone to giving a High Mass during class which was upsetting to the mostly Jewish students who registered for the course to aid in their preparation to become doctors or lawyers.

Witaker had wanted to begin a program in Chinese but was rebuffed by the Board curriculum committee when they suggested that first year Chinese be named Column One and the second year be called Column Two. He made a note to try again after the next elections.

The media center staff lacked imagination and had a general misunderstanding of their jobs. The two ladies, one a minister's wife, and the paraprofessional kept all journals current and tried very hard to be of assistance to students. However, they seemed to focus most of their time in keeping a watchful eye between the book stacks to prevent students from "frolicking." Even when they taught in the media center, one was always assigned to this watch so as not to soil their 10 years free of media center "frolicking."

They had proudly passed the record information on to the accreditation team during their visit. They received kudos in the final report but he had denied them their request to run "A Decade of Purity Lies Within" on the electronic message board outside the center. He sensed that an attempt would be made this year by either students or staff to end the record and that a live video feed of the event would be run over The School video system. Worse, he conjured that Evans might try to splice into the system one of his porno tapes using the center as a background. He made a note to have the media personnel visit other high school resource centers during the year.

The teachers selected to be advisors in extra-curricular activities were dedicated to their students. As a result, The School had an outstanding Student Council and Honor Society. Less fortunate were those students who chose to be involved in the Cooperative Work Experience program.

Mr. Wilson, who also taught Driver Education, often dropped off students at their place of employment using the school car, and he had been reprimanded for charging for the transportation service. Also, it was deemed inappropriate for students to be placed cleaning local taverns. He made a note to have one of the second year teachers begin certification to teach driver's education.

The Drama Club did two plays each year. Usually, one was benign such as *Our Town* while the other was more of a "to-day" performance. Last year's performance of *Chorus Line* proved to be an "outing" for several young men who had since graduated. He made a note to assist in selecting plays for next year.

The culinary arts program reaped state awards each year. The teacher/chef who ran the program was able to communicate and relate to students. Adorned in chef's clothing, they had a formal presentation four times during the year, one for the Board of Education prior to their monthly meeting. Knowing that the teacher/chef was busy in the range area, Witaker wisely assisted in monitoring the service before it left the kitchen and was able to prevent the presentation of a cheese ball in the shape of a penis.

The health service suite was staffed by two nurses. Miss Stevens was an older woman who had served as an Army nurse in Vietnam. She knew sick from sick and no one received any coddling from her. Girls with monthly cramps soon found themselves back in class and anyone with a cough got such a cold look that they left feeling better just because of the visit. She patched up the fighters brought in by the security staff, warning the staff that their manhood would suffer if they ever caused any of the blood on the student fighters.

Mrs. Jones, the younger nurse, was a nice lady with marital problems. She had a tendency to sob at any time, which was of great concern to any student having something removed from their eye. Thus, the applied education teachers had little difficulty in convincing students to wear safety glasses during class.

Special education was a bone of contention. Four of the teachers were assigned to in-class assistance with no more than five students each. Each also had a paraprofessional and two preparation periods. He disagreed with the dictates of the strong central office director and struggled to justify the expense of the program. He had assigned one of his assistants to sit in on Planning and Placement Team meetings and regretted having to do that to a good administrator. He did have a special place in his heart for the teacher and students in the severely handicapped class, one that he often visited to be reminded as to what special education really was all about.

Witaker liked the special education teachers. They were compassionate and dedicated to the students assigned to them. However, his vision of having each student become life-time learners by realizing the intrinsic values of learning was being offset by the M&M extrinsic rewards techniques of special education which was frustrating to him. He made a note to investigate who paid for the candy in their department.

Having had a good service experience, Witaker planned to submit a request to begin a ROTC program for next year. He liked the concept of a little spit and polish accompanied by some strict rules of conduct. He made a note to contact the Marines and Air Force in October and jotted it on his calendar.

Witaker related well with the five male teachers who also had military service experience. They talked the same language and handled discipline with ease. Their daily greeting of "How they hangin'?" always released some tension as Witaker walked the hallways. They were a great asset in assisting teachers who had classroom management problems in their departments. He made a note to buy two more cases of beer for his Labor Day picnic. The guys would be coming with their wives.

The faculty was mostly middle-aged with an average of 18 years of experience. With the exception of the untenured and new staff, all held at least a master's degree in either their area of expertise or another area of education. He had found that the older the personnel, the more likely they were to have fewer sick days and fewer classroom problems.

Personally, he liked them all and tried not to establish any favorites, but it was known that the "service guys" joked with him more than the others.

Listed as part of the professional staff was Wilford T. Whitemore III, Esq., the Board of Education attorney. Consider me part of your staff, Whitemore had told him at their first meeting, the former principal called me often except in his last year. The attorney advised him to make a pocket sized edition of Board policies and to carry it with him wherever he went. Witaker had not done so and had only called Whitemore once to make him aware that he had censored the student newspaper photographs of female students wearing thongs and had seized all the photos. Whitemore, III. Esq. requested all the copies for his files and seemed upset that Witaker had destroyed them. He made a note to have The Third deleted from the list of professional staff.

The School had four paraprofessionals not assigned to special education. They were assigned to tasks such as calling homes of absent students, assisting in rooms where substitutes were assigned, and clerical functions of varying sorts. The one problem that arose from their being in The School was they gossiped outside of the building. All of them had received their jobs via political appointments. Two were Democrat and two were Republican appointees and loved to tell tales of what the Mayor's son had done or about the teachers who may have been absent for shopping reasons. He made a note to have an assistant principal supervise them and work to have fewer stories leaving the building.

The cafeteria staff tried hard. Led by the nervous Mrs. Brown they provided less than wholesome meals which led to the most popular meal being Sloppy Joes until the student newspaper ran an article about a poll they had conducted indicating that the Joes were the favorite choice of hot lunch students. The headline read "Where is Your Cat Today?" Two years ago, using the pseudonym Mrs. Brown, the newspaper ran an article, "Keeping Your Weenies Warm," that led to Mrs. Brown having to take a leave of absence because of a meltdown. Of note was that Brown's Hair Nets won the girl's intramural basketball tournament.

The custodial staff was much different. Billy Evans had found a home in The School. He had made one of the storage rooms in the basement into his bedroom, had connected to the TV system and borrowed a TV and VCR and spent his nights watching porn films and blowing smoke rings from his "tokes" before going to bed in his makeshift motel room. He only left the school to refresh his pot supply and exchange films. His laundry was done in the home economics washer and dryer and he managed his meals from the cafeteria in exchange for assigning a work-study handicapped lad to scrub the ovens daily.

Evans kept himself in great shape with his evening workouts in the weight room and laps in the swimming pool. Although Witaker had the security staff do random searches of the boiler room and custodial area, they had not found either Evans' stash of films or hemp. He made a note to go with security on the next search, calculating that they may be participants in at least the watching of films, if they found them.

The school was staffed by 4 daytime custodians and 4 evening workers. One matron was assigned to clean the girl's lavatories and she slept most of the school day in the last stall in the second floor lav, and according to several girls who served as witnesses, passing gas whenever the bell rang.

The pool custodian position was the most desirable. He spent most of his day glued to the below the water level window watching the girls swim. He also received overtime for the swimming meets but worked only the girl's competitions, giving the boy's meets to Billy Evans so he could work out after everyone left.

The School was rife with nicknames. He was once called "BM" until several students in the honors program reminded the dyslexic boy who started the name that Mr. Witaker's last name began with a W rather than an M.

Miss Demster, a rather rotund biology teacher was Miss Dumpster. Several students had even painted Room 203 onto one of the cafeteria dumpsters, the number of Miss Demster's biology lab.

Mr. Wiles, the man he suspected as the one who drilled the hole in the English office when the English staff was attending a curriculum meeting, a botany teacher who assigned each student a fall project of collecting leaves from at least 20 different trees in the area, was known as the "leaf peeker." Miss Stevens, school nurse, was instrumental in discovering the identity of the "peeker" when Wiles visited her office with what he had thought as pink eye. Her diagnosis was that the damaged eye was caused by a strong cleaning solvent. In making the girl's lavatory into a female lavatory, the custodial crew washed the walls before painting and it was suspected that some of the solvent entered the "peeker's" eye as he scanned the room. It was reported that Miss Stevens rubbed her left index finger with her right one saying, "Shame, Shame, Shame!"

Al Jimonez, the custodian who cleaned the large boy's lavatory including the toilets and urinals and whose trousers always exposed some of his expansive butt was known as "UrinAL" or "Moon Pie."

The home economics teacher, June Prior, because of her tendency to show much of her superstructure was called "June Cleavage."

Because of seniority, the front desk was attended by the newest female employee. Not the most pleasant task because it was the first contact point for students sent there because of misbehavior, one Board of Education member's niece stood the watch. Her previous job had been at a favorite local pizza parlor so she had earned the label "Slice" and sometimes, "Anchovies." Slice had devised a system to lessen swearing by the incoming clients. When asked why they were sent to the office, students often responded with a phrase of their own or what they had said in class to warrant the visit.

Slice had laminated these phrases in a rolodex and the students could pick the appropriate one and hand it to her and she would pass it on to the dean. The students were aware of her system and quickly expanded their vocabulary which caused her to request additional files.

21

The dean began a numbering system which allowed students to pick the appropriate words and the most often selected was 69, even if it was uncommitted. Slice's job was to call parents to inform them of the offense and Brian did away with the system when several parents complained that they had received a phone call that their child had committed a 69 in a classroom.

"Balls" was Mr. Gooden. At the end of his PE class he required the students to retrieve all the used equipment and they would deliberately leave the basketballs in the gym until he reminded them by saying, "balls."

Paul Richard King, the dean of students had an 'i' and 'c' added to his initials between Richard and King. Being the dean meant handing out punishment and the students deemed it appropriate to name him "PRicK."

Mrs. Brown, the cafeteria manager, was named "Hash."

"Foreskin" was Joseph Bosko, a chemistry teacher. Because of his baldness and high forehead, "skin top" and "forehead" were shortened to his dismay. He had had the name for ten years when he began balding. When his wife found about his tag, she divorced him, not wanting to adopt his nickname prefaced by her Mrs.

Everyone in the applied education department had a name. The hands-on group had been tagged appropriately. Kevin Young, "KY," had earned his both with his initials and when the students substituted KY jelly into the gunk hand washing solution in the container in his metal shop. "R2D2," Mr. Wiggins, taught robotics. Mr. Butler, the automotive teacher, was called "Tranny," not because of his sexual orientation but that is what he called car transmissions. Students called his classroom "Condom Street" because his favorite phrase was, "this is where the rubber meets the road." The woodworking teacher, Walt Montgomery, was named "Dewalt," a combination of his name and his favorite brand of tools.

Though he knew of the nicknames, to Witaker they were Mr., Mrs., or Ms., but would dignify the comments whenever he heard the students anoint someone with a new tag.

Students, he reflected, would notice any weakness of staff and creatively attach a nickname to them which was passed down through the years. He hoped that he could remain professional and trusted enough to avoid any lifetime moniker.

Brian Witaker had a sense of humor and truly enjoyed the creativity of the students in tagging the staff. He had done much the same thing while serving in the Navy although the nicknames were much more vulgar in content. As long as the tags were not of a cruel or vulgar nature, he smiled inwardly whenever he overheard the students referring to staff by their non-formal names.

Having set the coffee timer in the kitchenette upon arriving, he rose to get himself his first of many cups for the day. The school bookkeeper had arrived and he chatted with her before returning to his office. He was most appreciative of having someone competent working with numbers, not his forte.

The secretarial/staff were professional and competent. They were respectful of the faculty and students and kept all the usual in-house conflicts to themselves, although he did hear an occasional slip when referring to "Slice." His own secretary, he had soon decided, was best at opening the mail so he did his own letters and memos. She presented herself well, had good telephone skills, and was a good source of local information for him.

The support staff worked hard on attending to the needs of the students. Guidance personnel awaited the onslaught of schedule changes, knowing that seniors would be in to drop out of Ms. McCann's class because she would be teaching Romantic Poetry which made her breathe hard.

The counselors spent much of their time in what they referred to as crisis intervention. Usually it meant putting verbal salve on first love break-ups. The guidance area was the main meeting place for students between classes as they tried to see who was coming out or going into the office, which gave them valuable information as to who was now "available" in the dating arena.

Social workers had already contacted their clients and met with parents, already nervous that the defensive parents were angry with over 180 days to go.

The school psychologist was compassionate, but had a general dislike of males. To her, they were all premature ejaculators.

Remedial staff only glanced at their schedule knowing they had the same students as last year while the special education staff would be counting the number of student assigned to them, their contract assuring them of only having 2 ADHD students each day.

The two assistant principals and dean were of a high quality. They had adapted to his leadership style and knew how to implement it. Witaker believed in being the true leader of the school and worked hard on having his vision understood. He was everywhere in the building during the school day and expected them to do so as well, knowing that students tended to get into trouble when there were no adults around.

During his first year they had successfully cut suspensions in half. They had jointly set a goal to reduce it even more this year. He knew the quality of the assistants would soon lead them to be a principal somewhere else and would work with them to make them better, as well. He had a noon meeting with them to get their input into the agenda he had written for the staff meeting tomorrow which preceded staff development. He also wanted to check with his assistant, who also served as the assistant athletic director, on the condition of the outside fields.

The security staff was a problem. They tended to see themselves as cops patrolling the hallways and seemed to keep count of the students they "busted." Even the smallest student who may have committed some minor school behavioral violation was made to do the "perp walk" to the security office. Statements were taken and they labeled every statement as a lie. Witaker had intervened countless times on behalf of the students and it irritated the security people. He made a note to have the dean more involved in training them to be more supportive rather than accusatory. They were good at breaking up fights and seemed to enjoy taking down both offenders with their style of intervention which they referred to as "a double arm bar crotch takedown." He had requested a female to be added to the staff and she would be arriving the first day of school. The current staff had already labeled her assignment as the Beaver Patrol.

The Memorial High School coaching staff was made up of faculty from within the building and other district schools. Within the conference, the teams were competitive.

The basketball coach, Angelo Frasciti, was annually selected as the conference coach of the year. It was noted that he always got the most out of his talent, despite a comparative size and athleticism deficit with the inner city schools in the conference. Witaker knew that Frasciti always ate his before game meals at the best Italian restaurant in town, having broccoli rabe and linguini with white clam sauce. His team did not want to play badly because he would remove them from the game, seat them and get in their face, loudly telling them what they needed to do. The heavy garlic smell made for superior play, the players not wanting to face the garlic breath. Even on a bad night, and after the garlic attack, they were forced to sit next to the coach whose digestive system now produced gas, made them request to get back into the game as quickly as possible. Coaching skills had nothing to do with his success. The two rows behind the team bench were always empty. His wife had left him, able to endure the first several years but the additional strain of state tournament games was too much for her olfactory system.

Prior to the construction of the building, a community wide contest was conducted to select a mascot and school teams' names. The contest resulted in three possible choices and a community wide vote was taken to make the final choice. The Screaming Eagles, The Beavers, and The Chargers were the selections.

Larry's Sports Bar patrons carried the selection of The Beavers because, unlike most elections, no one monitored how many times one voted. It was estimated that Shotsy Ritalli voted at least ten times, once after every shot and beer during the day. It was an unfortunate choice for the school, especially the cheerleaders. Through the Parent Council, Witaker had begun an initiative to have the name changed. He figured that Shotsy and the tavern guys had had enough laughs.

His office was small, room for the desk and chair, four arm chairs, two book cases, and a bulletin board. The attached lavatory was the size of an old telephone booth. It was a challenge to keep his neatly shined shoes dry while relieving himself. He spent little school time in the office, preferring to be out and about. He knew the best counseling occurred during breaks between classes and sought out those students who were not part of a group. Solitary kids were unhappy kids and he quickly learned their names and greeted them daily or chatted with them at their lockers.

He checked the Freshman list from guidance and the notes attached to it which gave him the names of those who would need his attention during the first week. He would have little trouble in finding the one with parrot colored hair.

Memorial High School had been built 22 years ago and he was the second principal of the building. JD Wilson, the principal Witaker had replaced, was a scholar who prided himself in developing a strong curriculum during his stay. Mr. Wilson was an office dweller, seldom seen by either staff or students. At graduation ceremonies, seniors often asked to have their picture taken with him because it was the first time they had seen him in their four years in the building. A kindly man, he had become very forgetful and timid in his last years. During his final year, JD arrived at school about 10 AM daily and left at noon, often forgetting where he had parked his car even though his space was clearly marked with a PRINCIPAL sign.

The secretary told Witaker that JD would go into the tiny office bathroom to "decompress" after any phone call and she made the mistake of mentioning it to one of the paraprofessionals. As a result, students used the pay phone in the auditorium lobby to call his private office number at 10 and 11AM. It was calculated that JD spent 99% of his last year in his lavatory.

One of the assistants ran the last graduation after discovering that the seniors had six cell phones in and around the podium and planned to call during JD's graduation address causing the poor man to decompress publicly.

JD Wilson moved quietly to Florida upon retirement taking the PRINCIPAL sign the staff gave him for a retirement gift with him, hoping he would be able to find his parking place in his new condo. Witaker made a note to have his secretary send a card to Mr. Wilson whose birthday was on Labor Day.

Upon reflection of the staff, Witaker found it was similar in many ways to the staff of the high school he had left to become the principal of Memorial. As a very successful assistant principal, he had many more informal meetings with the other staff, contacts that he missed as he attempted to set a very professional tone at his new school.

He made a note to be at his professional best, yet open, at the meeting with the new teachers and their mentors. Two of them already had a "deer in the headlights" look about them and he needed to assure all of them that the "boss" had their backs.

He had a concern for one of his second year teachers, Bill Desmond, who had linked up with Ms. McCann at the year end faculty picnic. After several glasses of wine, he was caught reading excerpts from Keats and Shelley to her. Two members of the department had to take the glassy-eyed woman home. He made a note to have a copy of Robert Frost poems placed into the young man's mailbox with a "cool-it" post-it attached to it.

Next on his checklist of things to do was a tour of the building with the head of district maintenance to insure that the building was ready for the opening of school He did a weekly walk-through with one of his assistants who was assigned to do any follow-up to items needing attention.

He took his maintenance folder from his Daily file and began to scan the data about the building.

Chapter Two

Middle Town was a growing bedroom town. Yet, it was one of the oldest in the state, receiving a charter in 1790. A building boom led to the decision to build a high school and what was calculated to be a savings in the long run from sending students to two adjacent towns for high school.

Another community, Middletown, came into existence in 1792. In allowing two towns with very similar names, the state government at that time didn't see a problem because they were at opposite ends of the state. In choosing the name for the school, and not be confused with an already existing Middletown High School, it was decided to avoid any political fallout and that The School should be in remembrance of those students who had given the ultimate sacrifice for their country. Thus, it became Memorial High School.

However, it was the first high school built in the community and no students had died on any battle fields. The large brass plaque on the main entrance awaited the first name and it made Witaker sad to know that one of his students would probably be the first name engraved on the empty honorarium.

The design of The School was an architectural delight from the front while the back was mostly cinder block. As construction of the building progressed, the Building Committee ran into money problems resulting in deciding not to implement the brick scheduled for the back walls resulting in most depressing rear surface. It was helpful that the back of the building was set into a hillside and only accommodated room for deliveries, dumpsters, and limited parking.

Even the homeless man who wandered the school grounds refused to set-up residence in the rear, stating that while homeless, he still had some sense of decorum and pride. Homeless Joe referred to The School as a "5", a great front and ugly rear. Witaker made sure that the man received a meal each day from the cafeteria, paying for it from his own funds. In return, the man had frightened off several attempts at vandalism at night. He made a note to give Joe the list of scheduled fire drills so that he didn't panic, thinking that the 1500 people leaving the building from different exits were trying to corner him and take his shopping cart.

Witaker was faced with the problems associated with a 22 year old building. Twenty year warrantees on the HVAC system and the roof had expired. JD Wilson had lost a year decompressing so it was left to Witaker to initiate a facilities study to get estimates of costs to renovate and upgrade.

The School had been cited for violations of the Disabilities Act, mostly in the pool area. Witaker had lost an appeal for one of the citations involving the diver's shower behind the diving board which had a one foot threshold at the entrance to keep the water from flowing onto the pool deck and was, thus, not wheelchair accessible. His logic that the school never had a diver in a wheelchair made no sense to the review board. The board also chastised him for suggesting that a ramp to the diving board would be very costly, not a suggestion made by the review team. To comply, Witaker had the shower shut down and the shower entrance enclosed in brick.

He also had to react to an OSHA violation in the cafeteria kitchen. One of the workers had been slightly burned when a pipe to the large steam kettle sprung a leak. Confused because Mrs. Brown said they never used the kettle, Witaker wondered why the kettle had not been shut down. Although unable to confirm his suspicions that Billy Evans used the kettle as his personal hot tub, he had the school plumber dismantle the kettle and remove it from the kitchen.

The flat tarred roof had lasted well over its 20 year lifetime. While there were some leaks around the air-conditioning units, the drains were clean and the surface well maintained thanks to Billy Evans who used the roof to sunbathe on weekends. Witaker had found a chaise lounge and cooler in the roof penthouse. He made a note to arrange any roof replacement or repairs around Evans' basking time.

The auditorium needed maintenance attention. Of the 1000 seats, most were in disrepair. Because so many parents and citizens attended school and community events in the auditorium, the town knew of its condition and he expected little difficulty in receiving support to upgrade that part of the building. The speaker system had so many splices that it was vulnerable to unauthorized use. During a performance of the town's drama club, someone had spliced in a country song, *I Won't Get Over You 'Til You Get Under Me*. It ruined a tender moment of the play.

The gymnasium area also would receive town-wide support in the need for upgrades. In design, the pool heating system was placed under the main gymnasium floor which caused the boards to rise during the winter months. Unfortunately, one of the raised areas was under one of the glass backboards and a ball hitting the area during a dribble might find a very high bounce. It had happened during one important league game last year.

With a tied score and ten seconds remaining in the game, one of the players from the other team stole a pass and was driving to the basket, the ball hit a high spot, hit him in the chin, and knocked him out cold. The Beavers recovered the ball and made the winning basket at the other end. The coach of the other team tried to contact the official to protest the condition of the court but they had left, laughing hysterically and happy that there wasn't any overtime. The protest to league officials was denied because someone had erased the last minute of the game's video tape.

The ventilation system for the locker room area had required immediate attention. Some work had been done during the summer. New fans were scheduled to arrive during the week and the towels blocking the ducts were removed. Students had discovered that by blocking the exhaust/return vent ducts and taking long hot showers that they could create an excellent steam room. Vent screens and the new fans would also help eliminate the fungus problem noted by the male PE staff.

The lobby of the main gymnasium always seemed dirty. The two public lavatories always smelled of smoke as patrons chose to smoke there rather than going outside in the cold during half-time of games. The glass enclosed trophy cases housed shelves of tarnished tokens of past successful teams. The small ticket booth over which "Stand Up For Your Team" was written, one of the Beaver's cheers, was the place of many encounters over the years. Witaker, during his first year, found that some students were referred to as "standup" boys or girls. He later found that it was in reference to what they had done in the ticket booth while the teams practiced. He made a note to a use the booth as a storeroom and sell tickets from a table outside of it for all future events. He also had wanted to replace all the lobby floor tiles until he found that they contained asbestos and so awaited the recommendations of the facility study.

The pool was a beautiful example of over design. The mosaic tile floor was in the blue and grey school colors, laid out so that they represented the lane markers. It was intended that there would be no need to have floating devices to signify lanes during swimming meets. However, over the years the chlorine had dulled the tiles making them almost seem the same color. Chaos resulted in a state tournament held several years ago as swimmers collided with each other, unable to discern which lane was theirs.

One glass block wall of the pool allowed outside light to enter, architects figuring that it would be a highlight during swimming events, never calculating that the meets would be held at night. The below pool observation window also was intended for coaches to watch swimmers and thus make recommendations as to how to improve their strokes or kicks.

As several swimming coaching changes occurred over the years, the current coach was unaware of the observation area. The pool custodian had the only key and he wasn't about to let the coach in on his private viewing spot. Wikater made a note to get the key from the pool man, change the lock and give the key to the new coach.

In design, the office areas, health suite, and the resource center had been air-conditioned. Over the past three years, two rooms off the resource center had been converted into computer labs. Last year when the roof units failed to cool these areas he discovered that the filters had never been cleaned. He wouldn't have known either except that the stench of several dead birds daily filled the center. At first he thought that Homeless Joe might have found a way into the building and was sleeping in the center, but his nose told him that the smell was not of a human nature.

Billy Evans didn't know he had to change the filters and the head of maintenance assumed Evans did it yearly. He made a note to have the head of maintenance pull all the maintenance manuals and make a computerized list of all required filter changes and convert it into a check list for the custodial staff. In addition, he noted, maintenance should order and have on inventory any needed parts to do so.

His list of notes had grown to two pages and he saw that Evans' name appeared on it many times. He knew he had to deal with the most important issues. Evans, the issue, would have to wait, the opening of school much more important at this time.

During his annual inspection, the Fire Marshal expressed concern about the chemistry lab. All the proper safety equipment was in place including an emergency shower, fire blanket, and safety glass cabinet but the preparation room had several strange containers. One capped bottle was labeled methane gas and another was a large mass of unlabeled material. Upon questioning, Mr. Sampson the teacher, explained that he was conducting a personal experiment to use the methane gas with the hypothesis that it may lead to being able to heat a neighbor's farm house. The unlabeled produce jar was a sample of the dung heap from the farm. Witaker had the bottles removed with a reminder to the teacher about pursuing personal agendas utilizing school facilities. He made a note to have the science chairman monitor his department more closely.

Brian Wikater took fire drills seriously. His Navy experiences made him aware of the dangers of fire and he had changed the fire drill procedures shortly after his arrival. Last year's first fire drill found students shuffling toward exits or teaming up with friends as they strolled casually to any door that led to sunshine.

The Fire Department arrived quickly, turned off their stop watches, jotted down their response time, and left. Inside the building, the cooks remained in the kitchen making Sloppy Joes, several teachers took a lavatory break in the faculty lounge, and one class didn't exit because the teacher was giving a pop quiz. It all changed as a result of a stern faculty meeting, procedural changes, and his sweep of the building during every drill. The Fire Department also took the drills much more seriously after he met with the Chief. The Chief had explained that the reason they didn't enter the building was that they didn't want to embarrass Mr. Wilson who was decompressing in his office.

The 240,000 SF building with 60 teaching stations was constricting current program needs. The original capacity of the building was 1200 students. Whoever had done the enrollment projections over 22 years ago should have ignored the birth rates and those moving into the community. He would have noticed that the young families were going to be prolific reproducers.

The core space, media center, auditorium, gymnasium, art and music areas, and cafeteria were adequate to meet the space needs. The number of classrooms, however, meant that teachers had to share rooms. Traditionally, the newer staff had a schedule that placed them in as many as three different rooms during a typical day. Witaker made sure that they understood the need to leave each room in clean condition after each class. He also noted that it was difficult enough as a beginning teacher and having to roam from room to room made it more confusing. He wanted to check the teacher's contract to see if he could assign the roaming to more senior staff. The movement might also be helpful to them in reducing their waistlines.

As principal he estimated that he walked at least three miles daily in his monitoring of the building and class visitations. Because the cafeteria Sloppy Joes reminded him of Navy SOS, he brought his lunch in every day, usually not eating it until after school was dismissed.

Smoking was prohibited in the school and on the school grounds. The policy created many problems, the most serious of which was for staff who still smoked. Knowing their needs, Witaker had assigned parking for them behind the school so that they could at least go into their cars to light up when they had a break. He had made no such adjustments for the students.

The outside security officer, a rent-a-cop, patrolled the parking lots and he prided himself on busting kids who were smoking outside or in cars. Standing all of 5'3" in his SWAT team boots that came to his knees, he hid behind cars, not needing to bend to be invisible. Although he could not carry a weapon, he wore a police belt with a holster. He had made his own water pistol using the butt of a real 9 MM pistol for the handle. The pistol was loaded with a bleach solution and he had used it once. Seeing what he thought was someone breaking into a car, he gave chase. His boots prevented him from fully bending his knees, so he tripped, pulled out his water pistol and "shot" the suspect who then disappeared. Later, with the help of the school security, they nabbed a lad with a large bleach stain on the back of his jacket.

However, the jacket was a denim motorcycle jacket that belonged to the boy's father. Because the boy had done nothing wrong except run, no charges were initiated. But, the boy's father came the next day wearing the jacket, drove through the parking lot on his Harley looking for the rent-a-cop who managed to avoid detection by hiding behind cars.

The rent-a-cop quit that day. Witaker made a note to contact the outside security company to check on who would be assigned to outside security for the coming school year.

The faculty lounge was, according to Witaker's Navy jargon, amid ship. The location was such that all teachers could drop in during unscheduled time. It was unofficially off limits to administration. It was the place where teachers became people and complained. Having been in lounges as a teacher, he knew the first order of business was to find fault. The pecking order was first administration, then students, parents, custodial services, testing, curriculum, and each other. At the end of the day it was strewn with empty lunch bags, dirty coffee/tea cups, newspapers, and the edited daily memo highlighting any grammatical errors with an occasional "Yea, sure" or "grievance?" marked in the margin.

Witaker had the lounge painted during the summer and had used most of his building discretionary money to buy better chairs and another refrigerator. He expected the complaints tomorrow to focus on the color of the paint, the discomfort of the chairs, and the brand of refrigerator. As he raised his pencil to make a note, he just smiled to himself and moved on.

The cafeteria was such that most of the "good kids" ate in the music room which was nearby. Mrs. Brown's attempt at providing food stations was a dismal failure. No one bought from the salad bar where fruit was also available. The pizza station served cold, stiff slices and was bypassed. The sandwich station, designed to be like a deli, was manned by a heavy lady who was referred to as "DWH" (Doesn't Wipe Herself) and therefore, left alone. It was back to the old serving lines for Brown's Hairnets this year.

He made a note to talk to Mrs. Brown about having DWH assigned to the dishwashing area.

He glanced at his watch and realized that he was behind schedule. He read his notes, went to the media center and borrowed a book of Frost poems, returned to the office and put the book into Bill Desmond's mailbox. The young teacher should get the message without any verbal contact.

Brian Witaker had learned early that good communication skills were necessary for successful leadership. Not everyone responded equally to either praise or correction.

He had told his faculty and staff that he had three styles of leadership: he could get out front and have them follow; he could suggest and have them work with him as a team; or he could get behind and kick butt. He now had to decide which approach to use related to the notes he had made.

Written communications were the first order of business as he prepared to end his day. To best get the results he wanted from Mrs. Brown regarding her cafeteria, he wrote a "hearts and flowers" memo hoping she had a restful summer, etc. He began his list of suggestions by asking, "Don't you think?" and added praise of her efforts in trying the food court program, although it was a dismal failure. Because she was so nervous in contacts with him, he ended the memo by telling her to go ahead and make whatever changes he suggested and telling her to simply email him if she agreed with his suggestions. He knew that she would agree with all of them.

Memorial High School's playing fields were a result of lack of foresight by the town. The town had purchased 50 acres of farmland on which to build the high school.

Over 100 additional acres were available but the town had not seen fit to purchase them at that time. The results were a very cramped playing field area.

Worst of all, west of the fields and school was a working dairy farm with cows and goats. The prevailing winds carried the farm odors onto the fields and into the school. As the farmer spread the manure to richen the hay and corn field soil, the early spring and late fall filled the air with his efforts.

The crusty old farmer took great offense when JD Wilson had approached him many years ago in an attempt to have him try chemicals on the fields rather than the odiferous organic compounds. That attempt caused the farmer to add the goats to his herd and to buy pig manure from a nearby farmer to double the organic warfare. The cagey old timer had cut the school schedules from the paper and would have the pig manure delivered precisely at the time of the annual Thanksgiving day football game or at the time of outside graduation exercises.

The old farmer had aged and did less and less farming himself as he turned over the work to his son. But the antagonism still existed. Witaker had sent a bottle of Jack Daniels to the old man last Christmas and the old fellow acknowledged the gift by sitting on his tractor last spring along the barbed wire fence near the baseball field. He had stopped the tractor, pulled out the bottle of Jack and took a slug as the baseball team watched. He held the bottle high and yelled, "Hey, Witaker, up yours!" Bribing the old guy was a failure.

The Football Fathers, a fundraising group for the football program, had organized an effort to replace the sod on the field. They were successful in collecting enough donations to replace the sod with synthetic turf. However, they figured to use any excess funds to start a concession stand inside the fenced field. As a result, and to save money on the new turf, they got the discounted item. It lasted only one year.

The new turf was flawed from the beginning. It expanded and contracted with the outside conditions which meant that it either had lumps in it or gaps between the layers.

The first game of use had enough large lumps that both teams used them as a trampoline during warm-ups. The Beavers quarterback was heard directing his wide receiver to cut toward the lump near the 20 yard line out-of- bounds line and stop five yards beyond it.

The opposing corner back tripped on the lump leaving the receiver wide open for a touchdown.

Coach DeBishop was wise enough to use the conditions of the field to assist his team in winning more than one game. The conference intervened and the turf was removed after only one year of use.

The artificial turf was taken off and grass replanted. The Football Fathers had noted the success the old neighboring farmer had in growing hay and contracted a load of his manure to be delivered in April to enrich the soil. They spread the manure by hand and the April showers made for one mess on the field. The clay content of the soil originally placed on the field had been taken from a nearby river bed. It had little percolation and even a light rain left puddles. Spring football practice that year had been one big mess of muddy clay and manure.

Finally, the field had been totally dug up and good soil brought in. It now was playable. But between the condition of the football field and the basketball court, Memorial High School was at the bottom of the places conference teams wanted to play.

Witaker prepared a memo to each of the teachers he wanted to observe the second week of school as a follow-up to his workshop on Teaching Techniques he was doing tomorrow. So as not to target them as "offenders," he included his service buddies on the list. He left the memo date open, scheduled each teacher on his calendar, personalized each memo with a positive comment, and put them in his outbox for delivery.

Observations can be traumatic for some teachers. He recalled one instance in his early teaching career when his district adopted a formal teacher evaluation plan. One teacher of 25 years quit when the principal showed up in her classroom with pad and pencil. She complained to the class that he was looking at her in a lewd manner and taking notes about her "B & Bs" (bust and buttocks). She put down the chalk, announced that she was quitting, and left the room and building. The totally surprised principal gave his notes to a girl sitting in the front of the class. He had simply written down the teacher's name and date. Ms. B & B got a position at a parochial high school and left that job as well when Brother James tried to observe her.

He called the outside security agency regarding the placement of an outside officer for the school parking areas. They gave him the name of the officer, his background, and the names of three references, one of whom was Billy Evans. Because he needed to talk to Evans about a multitude of things, he gave preliminary approval for the placement of the officer. He took the names of the other two references and put them into the folder for his assistants to call.

He trusted the head of district maintenance. As he called him with his notes, he knew each area of discussion would be investigated and corrected if needed. He asked for follow-up memos on each for his records and any accompanying suggestions.

Last year security cameras were placed in each hallway and center, north and south stairways. Only the first floor camera was activated and only he and his assistants knew the others were for prevention purposes only. The monitor was in the dean's office, but the students became suspicious that the stairway cameras were either down or fake when during senior week, six senior boys "mooned" the south stairway camera and no one responded. The event was observed and reported by the second floor custodian who told the dean in broken English; "Boys showed their ass on TV in stairway and I dropped bucket. I tink I know one because the others call him Harry Ass." Because Harry had graduated, the only identifiable perpetrator was gone. No money was included in this year's budget to connect more cameras so Witaker and the assistants would need to monitor the stairways more often.

Witaker placed his daily calendar in front of him. He wanted face to face contact of at least ten minutes with the young music teacher about his gyrations and attire. The young man had good potential, the students liked him, and he made his classes interesting for even the most reluctant kids. He just needed to understand that he wasn't one of them anymore. Witaker recalled an early experience with one of his young colleagues who became a "friend" of the students. They borrowed his Volkswagen beetle and left it deep in a back road culvert. The students denied taking the vehicle and it remained unfound until the Spring floods saw it floating down stream, eventually finding its way to the sewage treatment plant.

He scheduled a meeting for the next day with the computer technician to have all the business department computers double checked. Witaker needed to firmly establish with the technician that any faults with those units made them both vulnerable to the wrath of the business-like Ms. Wyant who ran the department. She was, he thought, the most consistent member of his staff. She disliked everyone, used all her sick and personal days, and never was one minute late in leaving. She kept grievance forms in her center desk drawer and used them at least twice during the year, always just before the winter and spring vacations. They always involved time because her mantra of "time is money" overwhelmed her.

Ms. Wyant arrived and left department head meetings exactly on time, taking shorthand notes while most of the others used a lap top. Her goal, it seemed, was to make everyone as miserable as she. She was unsuccessful as evidenced by the faculty group picture which showed all with smiles except for her.

Witaker had to meet with Mr. Wiles and wrote his name on the schedule for tomorrow. He had a growing concern about this otherwise competent teacher who was prone to peeping. Wiles was worth salvaging and Witaker wanted to let him know that he was aware of his "urges." He had obtained the name of a psychiatrist in another community who, he hoped, would help Wiles. He also wanted Wiles to know of his value to the school and students. This meeting would require a soft and caring approach and Witaker wanted to talk to the school psychologist to get her input before he met with Wiles.

Witaker doubled-checked with his secretary to make sure that both coffee and pastries had been ordered for the first faculty meeting in the morning. Because dress for the first meeting was informal as teachers set-up their rooms after the meeting, Witaker contacted the assistants and the dean. All administrators would be wearing ties and jackets to set a formal tone for the positions they held.

Brain Witaker looked over his list one more time, arranged his desk in an orderly manner, and completed the agenda for the faculty meeting in the morning. He deliberately made the first several items very serious ones and the last several light and humorous. Teachers, like their students, tended to have short attention spans and he wanted them to remember the priorities of the meeting.

Two aides and a part-time summer custodian had finished distributing the textbook orders. Witaker's walk-through into each teaching area noted that all had been cleaned, the floors waxed, and new textbooks were placed on desktops for easy teacher inventory. The pianos had been tuned, band uniforms and choral gowns pressed and hung, the gym floors resurfaced, and all the trophies in the gym lobby display case had been shined. He had tested the communications system, fire alarm, and the clock system.

Each staff member had a booklet with all assignments, schedules, class lists, and other pertinent school information ready for distribution after the faculty meeting. He had learned not to give the booklet out before the meeting, the staff paid more attention to it and less to him during the meeting. He was ready for return of the staff and the beginning of the school year.

Chapter Three

Brian Witaker arrived at The School at 6 AM on the first day of the return of the faculty and staff. After starting the coffee and paging Billy Evans on the intercom, he started his computer and the copy machine.

By the time Evans arrived, Witaker had poured his first of many coffees for the morning. Evans looked fit and tanned as he entered the office wearing cut-off dungaree shorts and a T-shirt saying "The Yankees Suck!" Evan's flip-flops were wet indicating his morning swim had been interrupted by the page.

Before tomorrow, Witaker knew he had to address the myriad of problems associated with his head custodian, but now was not the moment. He directed Evans to open all the windows in the cafeteria, turn on the air-conditioning in the auditorium, and to lock all entrance doors except the main one.

Witaker wanted no unwelcome visitors during the day and he remembered the problems JD Wilson had several years ago when some students guided a goat herd from the neighboring farmer's pasture into the first floor hallways The newspaper headlines and accompanying pictures made for a disruptive first day for the students, particularly the one of a billy goat and a nanny mating with the English department bulletin board in the background extolling Romantic Literature.

Witaker directed Evan to change into the uniform provided to the custodial staff and to make sure that the rest of the custodians also dressed in their uniforms. Evans gave an "Aye, Aye" and departed. Evans demeanor made for a bad beginning for the principal as he pulled out the agenda for the first meeting of the morning.

Evans' inappropriate attire was connected to the first agenda item. At the June meeting of the Board of Education, they had adopted a dress code policy for students. The new policy was referred to by the staff as the "C" policy for crack and cleavage. It seemed that the teachers' association initiated discussion of the policy because many of the staff were upset with seeing too much of the males' butts and too much of the females' super structure. It had taken all of last year to implement a no hat policy and Witaker suspected the worst for the new one.

The new dress code policy had been published several times in the newspaper and Witaker had mailed a copy to all the parents. The policy was vague and subject to interpretation. Simply stated it said, "At no time should any part a student's anatomy below the shoulders be exposed to view."

Witaker's office had been bombarded with phone calls all summer. He had written a response for the clerical staff to handle the calls. His interpretation was that T-shirts could be worn with no vulgar statements on them, all shirts were to be tucked in, all pants were to be a waist level, and that the policy did not include hands, arms, or ankles.

He needed to re-affirm his interpretation with the staff at the meeting. He knew that Judy "Jugs" Benoit would be the first to be sent home tomorrow and he wanted the female assistant principal to be the one who intercepted her upon entering the building. He would handle Julio Martinez himself.

He didn't anticipate any protesting about the policy before the beginning of school but had requested two policemen to be on the grounds directing traffic upon arrival of the buses and student cars. Security personnel had also been alerted and had communications connections with the policemen on duty.

Witaker had scheduled the two new teachers to meet with him and his assistants at 7 AM. An assistant was assigned to guide each one and they would be meeting their mentors from their departments later in the day. His calm reassurance, he knew, wouldn't really lessen the excitement they were experiencing, but he wanted to let them know that the structure was more than enough to support them. Unfortunately the new teachers would have a roaming schedule because the teacher contract honored seniority in room assignments. Unless a senior teacher stepped forward to exchange room assignments with them, the 22 year-old "kids" were floaters.

At 7:15 he met with the school psychologist to discuss a plan to assist Mr. Wiles address his problems. Wiles, according to the female psychologist, posed no problems for the students. She also noted that he must be a premature ejaculator, which was information of no use to Witaker. Mr. Wiles was a good teacher with an excellent background and related well to the students until they found out about his problem.

Witaker hoped that the summer had made memories weaken so that Mr. Wiles might begin the year without being subjected to ridicule from the students. Though he hoped so, Witaker didn't really think it would be so. Witaker had placed Mr. Wiles on evaluative assistance which meant he was in jeopardy of losing his job. Witaker truly hoped that seeing a psychiatrist on a regular basis might help. Brian Witaker fully expected to have to release the man before the end of the first term, but he felt he owed the man the opportunity to succeed.

At 7:30 he met with Mr. Wiles and the psychologist and laid out a plan which included a twice a week meeting with the psychologist and weekly reports from the psychiatrist. To prepare for the worst, Witaker had interviewed two botany/biology teachers as a possible replacement for Wiles and had selected one to be a permanent substitute.

As he left his office to go to the auditorium, one of his Navy veteran teacher buddies, Bill Soden, noticed the new teachers leaving the office area and greeted Witaker with, "New folks, Skipper?" Soden had been a submariner and knew the importance of training new personnel as quickly as possible.

Witaker responded, "Yes, and you got one of them to mentor. Make the new souls as good as you." They gave each other a quick walking salute and moved on to the auditorium for the meeting.

As always the two hundred plus people were spread out in the seats, usually sitting with department colleagues. On four tables entering the auditorium, piles of booklets and schedules were guarded by the clerical staff. The only handout was the agenda.

Clad in summer attire, the exited staff settled down as Witaker entered. Billy Evans had cooled the area and rested in the back upper level of the auditorium in full custodial uniform as he screened the females as they passed by.

Quiet settled in the room. Witaker began, "If you were students, over half of you would be sent home tomorrow for violation of the new dress code policy. But we are not students. We are professionals and will dress that way with shirts and ties for the men and professional attire for all the females. We will model the policy for the students, parents, and the public." He had set the tone for the meeting and the year.

His military service buddies sitting together smiled and gave him a sitting salute. He had everyone's complete attention and quickly moved through the agenda

Successful leaders vary their styles depending upon situations and circumstances.

Witaker preferred to use a team approach when addressing most school related initiatives. He sought input and used it in guiding curriculum development and school regulation changes. However, he knew that in difficult situations he needed to be out front leaving no questions as to who was in charge and held responsibility. The delicate new dress code policy was one such situation. He alone was the one who would be held accountable for the success or failure of the Board's decision. He was up to it, even if he didn't totally agree. The Board didn't want students to expose butts or cleavage and he was the man in charge of having the student body cover their privates. In female-sensitive cases, he would use the judgment of his female assistant to guide him and would let her determine policy violations of that gender. But he would handle and take any phone calls from parents who might disagree with her judgment and associated discipline.

Witaker kept the end of the agenda light and humorous. His keen sense of humor and ability to remember jokes made him a popular speaker and presenter. The School was a great source of funny events and he related them to the staff. He never made light of students and the jokes were always on him or the staff. Even Mrs. Brown from the cafeteria giggled with a nervous twitch to her nose.

The last two agenda items were informational. He reminded them of his Teaching Techniques presentation and mentioned the forthcoming state testing, an item for every staff meeting to come.

Witaker introduced the new members of the faculty and the 45 minute staff meeting was over. Henceforth, all of his staff meetings would follow a set pattern of lesson design he wanted the teachers to follow in their classrooms and so he modeled it when he met with them.

As the meeting ended, the two mentors moved toward the new teachers and led them into the lobby. They would be with them most of the day having them assist in setting up the mentor's room, a luxury the new teachers did not have. They also would walk them through their schedules and show them the rooms in which they would be working. They and the new teachers would not have to attend the Teaching Techniques program, it would be too much for the new people to absorb in one day.

Witaker knew that one of the new teachers, Ms. Ledbetter, would quickly be given the tag of "Ms. Bedwetter." So when he had recommended her for employment, he had suggested that she start the year using her soon-to-be married name instead. She understood and agreed and he had introduced her using her future husband's last name. He had made arrangements with the assistant in charge of scheduling to have her married name on all the schedules. He secretly hoped that her fiancé didn't get cold feet before the Columbus Day weekend wedding. The central office knew and would take care of the state certification requirements and not mess up her pay.

The School office was crowded with parents and new students registering for school the next day. Despite four newspaper articles informing parents of the need to pre-register students so that they would have an opening day schedule, many just waited until the last minute. For some students not bearing records, it would be several days before they could be placed into classes. He also noted that the Hispanic translator was very busy talking to parents. It appeared that the bilingual program would be full. He talked to one of the clerical staff and make sure that each new student received a copy of the new dress policy written in several languages.

As a past assistant principal, part of Witaker's responsibilities was to discipline students who had somehow violated school policies. However, he never quite got it right when Hispanic students were sent to him for "inappropriate language." The teachers had no knowledge of Spanish but assumed that when the students addressed them with a certain look and body language that they were cursing. Also, the teachers were not able to tell him what they had said because of the language barrier. Thus, Witaker usually just told the students to speak English when talking to the staff.

To better understand the language when he became the principal of The School, Witaker had utilized the questionable talents of Mr. Sanchez to conduct a workshop on inappropriate Spanish language. While the staff learned some phrases, most suspected than Sanchez used the time to insult some of the staff in Spanish by talking too quickly for anyone to understand. Witaker had taped the workshop and gave a copy to the assistants and the dean. At least they had some knowledge when Hispanic students were sent to them for "inappropriate language."

As the new students were registering, Witaker heard one of the mothers curse in Spanish to the clerical staff. He stopped and told the mother in English that her language was inappropriate and asked her to apologize. The mother was impressed that he knew Spanish and tendered an apology in English to the clerk. When her son standing nearby asked the mother who he was she answered, "El Hombre." He indeed was, but wished that Sanchez could have been there to reply to the mother in his own special way.

El Hombre walked into his office. Awaiting him was a sobbing Ms. Ledbetter. After gathering herself, she explained that her engagement had been terminated by her fiancé when he discovered that she was using his name for school purposes. Witaker suspected that the guy was looking for a way out and that he, Witaker, had provided it for him.

Ms. Ledbetter's grief turned to anger as she continued to explain her demise. It suddenly occurred to her that the whole sad situation was the fault of Witaker. Had he not tried to help she would still be on target for marriage. Between sobs, she loudly told El Hombre that she was resigning. She could not possibly work under a man who had destroyed her life. She scribbled a resignation note and signed it, throwing it onto his desk and left his office.

Witaker sat for a moment thinking that the former fiancé had made a good decision. He called the central office informing them that Ms. Bedwetter, excuse me, Ms. Ledbetter, had resigned. One of the permanent substitutes now was a full time teacher and would replace the angered woman. He made a note to contact the Board attorney to let him know of the entire circumstances should Ms. Ledbetter bring suit against him for mental anguish, etc. Trying to be a good guy could have drastic consequences and he suspected that he had not heard the last of Ms. Ledbetter.

Witaker called the assistant who handled scheduling and made arrangements to have Ms. Ledbetter's schedule changed to that of the permanent substitute. It would be done before school opened in the morning.

El Hombre had an hour before the Teaching Techniques workshop. He glanced at his watch just as the union representative entered his office. Mrs. Petrone was an aggressive union rep. He could count on her coming into his office at least twice a month. Being an English teacher, she either had a complaint against some directive or about the grammar in his memos. Witaker was fortunate to have made friends with her husband who had done some contracting work in The School. Mr. Petrone would call Witaker from time to time letting him know that it was Mrs. Petrone's PMS time. Thus, they both awaited an explosion.

Mrs. Petrone explained that several of the female staff took exception to his remarks about how they were dressed this morning. Because she tended toward the matronly style of dress, Witaker knew the complaints came from two younger female teachers in her department. Witaker calmly apologized if some took offense at his remarks but all needed to know what they were facing regarding the dress policy. It appeased the union rep enough to cause her to smile.

The union rep left, but he expected to see her again once everyone had read their schedules. It always happened, someone felt they had drawn the short end of the scheduling stick. Last year it had been a pregnant teacher who needed more breaks for the bathroom and the schedule had her teaching three classes in a row. Because it was near the office, he had taken the beginning of her third class so that she could accommodate her bathroom needs. He did not receive a thank you from either the teacher or Mrs. Petrone. They must have figured that he had enough free time while they worked their demanding schedules.

Mr. DeBishop, the football coach, knocked on his door. He was a PE teacher who was in constant conflict with the athletic director. A good coach, except for an occasional "F" bomb on the field, expected an off-year for his squad. The team was young and inexperienced. He had an untested junior quarterback who flinched at the line of scrimmage who an opposing linebacker yelled at him. The young flincher was the son of a local politician and the coach was under duress to play the poor young man. The lines on the coach's face indicated that he had some problems to relate to his boss.

The coach berated the AD for getting truck tires rather than car tires for the team to run through, thus creating some groin strains for the younger boys. After complaining about an increase in team jock itch, he finally got to the real problem. The Football Fathers, a fund raising group for the team, had gotten into a knock-down brawl at their last meeting.

The Fathers were split between being democrats and republicans, and having a lad playing quarterback who had a democrat dad, made for tremendous tension. When coach DeBishop told them he would play the best player, despite political affiliation, the republican father of the backup quarterback, decked the starting quarterback's father and it turned into a political brawl.

Coach DeBishop was a strong man, but he told Witaker, he couldn't break up the fight. Two men were taken to the hospital and the town dentists would be busy repairing several others. Now the boys on the team were equally split and filled with young testosterone and eager to revenge the fathers who had been cold cocked at the meeting.

Coach DeBishop asked Witaker to intervene. They scheduled a meeting with The Fathers, but Witaker told the coach that he and his assistants would have to handle the squad. If they could successfully bring peace to the older men, the kids would follow. That the police had not been involved in the brawl meant that they probably could bring some sense to the older guys. It was going to be a long season for the coach and team.

As the coach rose to leave he told Witaker that the assistant coaches called the young quarterback JD. They were the lad's initials but they used them in context of old JD Wilson, the timid former principal. It indeed was going to be a long season for the coach.

A few minutes after the coach left, the AD knocked at his door. Joe Ritalli had gotten the AD job four years ago when his father was the mayor. His qualifications were questionable, but JD Wilson gave up the fight when it was evident that the Board would appoint Ritalli even if Wilson did not recommend him. Ritalli had been a fourth grade teacher who had failed several times for principal openings and now held a full-time administrative position with an office and secretary.

Known as "Beans" by the other athletic directors because he always referred to the money split between the two schools as Beans, Ritalli saw his position as one of power. Beans was disliked by every coach in every sport. Even his secretary disliked him and continually signed for any secretarial opening in the district.

Joe Ritalli came to report the brawl. His slant, as he gave the details to Witaker, was that Coach DeBishop was to blame. Ritalli had not been at the meeting but had heard about it from his political buddies. The political take on the meeting was further confirmed by Shotsy, Joe's cousin, at Larry's Sports Bar when Beans had stopped for his morning "coffee." Beans always smelled of alcohol and his red nose gave away his weakness.

The AD wanted Witaker to suspend the coach indefinitely for initiating the fight.

Witaker had had prior dealings with the AD and knew he was a bully and a coward and Brian Witaker was in no mood to support the man he had come to disrespect for his treatment of the coaches.

Witaker stood over the seated AD and said, "I know what happened at the Football Fathers meeting and Coach DeBishop did everything he could to stop the conflict. And if you come into my office again smelling of alcohol, you will be the one suspended. Further, if you can't build affirmative relations with the coaches within one month, you will be placed into the assistive evaluation program. You will receive a memo from me by the end of the week informing you of the expectations you will need to address and you will respond to me in writing as to how you will do it. Now, leave my office and go home. I don't want you to take your anger out on your secretary."

The AD paled and left. It was just another problem that Witaker had to address but he had given himself enough time to do so. He knew he was in for a political battle and needed to document everything, so he made notes of the meeting as he gathered his own temper. Anger was enemy number one.

Slice entered his office as he was writing. One of the boys registering was from Portugal. He was 15 years-old and had not been in school for two years. He had been working on a fishing boat and carried a knife in a sheath on his belt. State law required him to register for school because of his age. Witaker called the social worker and gave her the assignment of finding the young man an "internship" on a fishing boat at the nearby fishing docks.

As he rose to move toward his Teaching Techniques workshop, Mrs. Thiesman, the art teacher appeared at the door. She wondered if the new dress policy would apply to the nude model she had planned for her first marking period drawing class. Also, her room needed four more tables because the class size for the drawing class had grown to 22 boys.

The entire boys' soccer team had registered for the class. They had inside knowledge of her plan for a nude model. Mrs. Thiesman, a young widow, was dating Mr. Santos, the head soccer coach. Santos had alerted the boys calculating that she could schedule the model on the day the team was playing their biggest rival. Since the class was the first period, the boys would have time to recover from the experience but the testosterone would still be at a high level.

Neither Mrs. Theisman nor Brian Witaker knew of his plan, but Witaker was suspicious as to why the boys had suddenly become art students. Brian Witaker calmly explained to widow Thiesman that her plans to have a nude model must be changed. The live model, he said, must be fully clothed and meet the requirements of the new dress code. He also instructed her to change the description of the drawing class cited in the course selection booklet to state that all live models would be fully clothed.

Mrs. Thiesman was obviously disappointed, but seemed to understand. Witaker noted that the soccer team was in for a big disappointment as well. The downcast team would probably suffer the loss of hormones which would make it more difficult in their quest for a conference championship.

Witaker again started toward the door for his Teaching Techniques workshop. But Pete Dinato, head of district maintenance was coming in. The district maintenance staff had arrived early to oversee the re-keying of the building before the opening of school. The new locks would allow more control of keys because it seemed that everyone had a master key. Witaker suspected that even Homeless Joe could access the building. The re-keying was well behind schedule. It should have been done early in the summer, but difficulties in getting a new budget meant waiting until the funding was confirmed.

Dinato had a concerned look on his face. Mr. Wiles had approached him requesting to borrow a portable drill with a concrete bit on it. Dinato had told Wiles that the maintenance staff would be happy to drill whatever he needed, but Wiles insisted that he could do it on his own. Dinato reported that Wiles was last seen heading toward the supply closet adjacent to the female staff lavatory.

Witaker's shoulders sagged with the information and thanked Dinato for his "heads-up." Witaker would have to deal with Mr. Wiles later. Now he had to do the Teaching Techniques workshop.

Witaker began to feel a little like JD Wilson as he left the office. His open door policy had lent itself to the problems of the others, but he had some time to react to most of them. As he left he directed Slice to arrange a meeting with the school psychologist after the workshop.

Witaker was able to present a workshop on wrong teaching techniques. He asked that no one take notes, just observe and to be prepared to give him feedback on the presentation.

Remarkably the attendees had a grasp on good teaching techniques and gave a knowledgeable account of what he had done wrong. After listing the imperfections on a white board,

Witaker placed correct methods next to the wrong ones. The attendees copied the list and Witkaker asked each of them to write a time for him to visit their rooms next to their names on the signup form. He instructed them not to give him a date until October. He would have his hands full until then.

The cafeteria was full as the staff ate lunch. Passing by, Witaker noted that Mrs. Brown had done herself proud. She had even assigned DWH to the dishwashing room.

The cafeteria staff wore red, white and blue hairnets and formed a semi-chorus line and began singing the song from *Welcome Back Kotter*. He hoped it wasn't a rehearsal for tomorrow's lunches. The shocked staff acknowledged the performance with light applause except for Albert Sanchez who stood and grabbed his crotch like Michael Jackson and lip synched the words. His response got heavy applause. Mouths agape, the new teachers had a scary look in their eyes. Witaker knew he had to do damage control for the cafeteria experience the young people just witnessed.

Arriving in the office, Witaker asked Slice to have Mrs. Brown meet with him later in the afternoon. Hash had been playing the piano while the hair-netted ladies did their low kicking routine.

The school psychologist awaited him in his office. Witaker explained what had happened to Mr. Wiles as reported to him by Pete Dinato. She met the news with furrowed brows and began shaking her head up and down as if she knew the cause of Wiles' behavior. "I believe I told you earlier," she said, "Wiles is a premature ejaculator. Men like him never respond to help. I'm willing to bet he never finished drilling the hole either."

Witaker knew Mr. Wiles was a lost cause. He thanked the psychologist and she left shaking her head. He seemed to be the only one willing to help the man and it wasn't going to work. The leaf man had to go today.

Chapter Four

Billy Evans sat just above the exit stairway as the morning staff meeting had ended. He followed the crowd as they entered the lobby to receive copies of their schedules. He slyly requested a copy of the media center schedule, explaining that he needed to assign custodians to the area. He said that the schedule would allow them to clean when no one was assigned to the media center.

Mrs. LeClair worked as a part-time clerk and she had known Billy Evans since he was a little boy in the neighborhood. He had been a smart boy who always was looking for a way to do things as easily as possible. He could have been a success at whatever he had chosen, she thought, but it just wasn't his way. His intelligence had gotten him to the top of the custodial list, but she was suspicious of his motive for asking for a copy of any schedule. She made a note to let Mr. Witaker know that Evans wanted the media center schedule. Evans was up to no good, her mind told her. He had some sort of plan that the principal needed to investigate. She called the office and quickly gave the information to Mr. Witaker. He is smarter than Evans, she thought, and he will find out what Evans was up to.

At 1 PM, after completing her work schedule, she went to the office. She wanted to remind Mr. Witaker of the Billy Evans schedule request. She knew Witaker was a busy man but she just felt it was important.

Chapter Five

The morning had been hectic for Brian Witaker and the afternoon was about to become busier. He nibbled on the pizza sent to him from the cafeteria. He had just met briefly with Mrs. LeClair and agreed with her assessment that Evans was up to something. He just needed a little time to investigate.

Mrs. Brown would be coming in after the lunch mess had been cleared. He had to meet with Mr. Wiles in a most difficult situation. The conclave of teachers sitting at the table where the senior-most staff had gathered for lunch indicated that many would be in to discuss their schedules. But his biggest concern was the re-keying of the building.

Witaker could see the front of the building from his office window. The lock company trucks were no longer to be seen. They had started re-keying all the inside locks and he was in possession of a new key for his office and Slice had the key for the main office. But he had not yet received a master key for the building. The maintenance department truck no longer was on the grounds as well. He hoped that they had just gone to lunch.

Barging into his office came the angry head of the business department. The computer system had been checked and all was working well. She began her tirade, "Can you imagine?

They left all the printers without any paper. Who is going to put paper in my printers? And they left finger prints on the monitors. Who is going to clean those off? I don't expect you to answer, you'll just say it is our job. But, see if you can find that in our job description! The computer people had no business making a mess of my business department. We never had any problems when JD Wilson was here. I know someone will be sick tomorrow from our work overload!"

Witaker started to respond, but Ms. Wyant turned and left. He told Slice to make sure that a substitute would be available for tomorrow for the business department.

A glowing Mrs. Brown came in on schedule. She was truly proud of the song and dance recital during the staff lunch. She had gotten the piano from "that nice music man" and had practiced *Welcome Back Kotter* for several hours in a music practice room. She had even been able to use the foot pedals and had only one mishap when her foot slid off a pedal caused by a piece of slippery lettuce on the bottom of her rubber soled shoes. She awaited praise from her boss.

Witaker smiled. He didn't want a Hash Brown meltdown before school even started. She had done all that he had asked in his "hearts and flowers" memo. Nor did he want to have a repeat performance of the chorus line recital tomorrow. He had thought of a way out.

But before the could begin, Mrs. Brown proudly announced that the cafeteria staff was making cookies for the staff lounge each day and would have them placed in a doggy shaped cookie jar she had found in the garbage.

Bells went off in Witaker's head! Earlier in the summer he had been stopped by Ms. Aphros who taught philosophy. When her pet terrier passed to his great reward, she had Tinkles cremated and his ashes put into a doggy shaped cookie jar on a shelf behind her desk. It held the most important spot just above the busts of Aristotle and Plato. On her return from her summer trip to Greece she came to get Tinkles. The jar was gone. Apparently the summer cleaning crew had emptied his remains and threw the jar away. Mrs. Brown had taken it from the garbage and now it contained sugar cookies in the staff lounge.

Even though DWH had cleaned it well, some of old Tinkles ashes must now be in staff digestive systems. Witaker stifled a laugh and thought, wait until Ms. Aphros goes into the lounge!

Mr. Witaker profusely thanked Mrs. Brown for all her efforts and creativity in initiating the chorus line bit. However, he pointed out, Board of Education policy prohibited any performance to a gathering of more than 200 people unless both and fire and police services were on the premises. He had not budgeted for the event and thus it had to be postponed.

While disappointed, Mrs. Brown accepted the reasoning. He asked her if he could have the doggie cookie jar for his office explaining that it would be a great feature for visiting parents who he saw almost daily.

He again thanked her and she left, reappearing several minutes later with the cookie jar. He summoned Al Jimonez, "Moon Pie," to the office and told him to take the jar to the boiler room and fill it with ashes from one of the boilers. When Ms. Aphros left her room, Witaker instructed him to place the jar back on the shelf above Aristotle and Plato. He made a note to buy another doggy cookie jar over the weekend and hoped that Moon Pie knew who Aristotle and Plato were.

Brian Witaker was putting band aids on the small wounds and giving himself time to address the larger ones. He awaited the influx of those who had time to study their schedules. He only would see those who had not been satisfied with a meeting with the assistant principal who did the scheduling. From his experience, they would come in pairs and perhaps have Mrs. Petrone, the union rep, with them.

The first two came soon after Mrs. Brown departed, having dropped off the cookie jar. He seldom had problems with the science department. They were too busy getting their rooms ready and planning their year. But Mr. Vandervort and Mr. Carney seemed to have some concerns about the scheduling and respectfully entered the office.

Mr. Vandervort usually taught the biology Advanced Placement course and Mr. Carney had senior Physics. Through some scheduling snafu, Mr. Wiles had been scheduled for the biology AP and Ms. Lamphier, a new teacher, had been assigned senior Physics.

Because the assistant principal knew of Mr. Wiles difficulties, she had sent the two onto Brian Witaker. Witaker quickly made a note to his assistant to correct the problem, relieved that it was a simple one.

The two thanked Mr. Witaker and turned to leave. Mr. Carney had one comment upon leaving that raised Witaker's interest. He told Witaker that a TV/VCR mobile stand had been taken from his room and he thought it might be Billy Evans who was seen pushing one down the hall and disappeared in the area of the custodial supply room.

Why, Witaker thought, would Evans be taking an AV cart into a custodial supply room? That room was the domain of the female custodian that Evans hated. Witaker needed more time to analyze the movement.

Waiting outside his office were two history teachers. Mrs. Anzalone and Mr. Vitalli had adjacent rooms. They usually taught US History and Ancient History. Mrs. Anzalone had come from Atlanta with her husband and seldom got beyond the Civil War. She always got emotionally involved in Sherman's march and would literally shake when describing the devastation. The students knew of her southern connection and would stand and cheer for Sherman when she tried to explain the pain the Georgia folks still felt from the victorious march.

Mr. Vitalli had only six students for his one Ancient History class. He never realized that ancient history to the students in front of him were World War II, the Korean War, and the Vietnam War. To them, Helen of Troy was the hooker who worked on the corner of Troy and Grand Streets. The main problem was that Mr. Vitalli was a dry as a pop corn fart and his class was a "sleeper," according to the students.

But their scheduling problem was one of time. The required US History courses for sophomores were to meet during the first period and the elective Ancient History course was scheduled for the last period. First period classes were the worst, most of the students were still groggy. The last period found many on the nod wanting a nap and Mr. Vitalli's dry and slow delivery was the sound of a gurgling brook in their ears. He often was interrupted by snores and didn't have the nerve to wake the sleeping students; he just kept on hoping that his excitement for the Romans would awaken them. It didn't.

Mr. Witaker wondered why the two had come to his office. Then he realized that the assistant in charge of scheduling wanted him to tell them that the first and last periods were just as important as the ones in between. He did, and they left and heard Mrs. Anzalone say something like "Damn Yankee." Mr. Vitalli whispered something to her which sounded like "Khan" to Witaker. He ignored both as he looked outside his office to see Mr. Sanchez and the Latin teacher awaiting their turn.

Brian Witaker reached into his desk and took out a bottle of aspirin. He gulped two of them down and waved the Foreign Language people into his sanctum.

Chapter Six

Pete Dinato's watch showed 1 PM as he awaited the return of the lock company. They had re-keyed every inside lock and had given master keys to him and Brian Witaker. They hadn't started the outside and were well behind in their work.

The three men assigned to the task had left before noon. Dinato suspected that they had taken advantage of Larry's Sports Bar special of beer boiled hot dogs with sauerkraut accompanied by a pitcher of tap beer for $3.95 per person. The head of maintenance got into his van and headed to the bar. In the parking lot he saw the lock company truck just as he had suspected. The special was too much for them to ignore.

Upon entering the bar, Dinato saw Shotsy Ritalli and the three man crew. Two of the men were throwing down shots of cheap whiskey along with beer chasers. Shotsy was cleaning up on their generosity as Larry took money from the cache on the bar in front of one of the workers. The two were well on their way to oblivion.

Shotsy greeted Dinato who he knew from their school days. Both had been fair athletes and remained connected from time to time after softball games. "Just getting ready for the hurricane," Shotsy said. "We need to oil our motors before the rain rusts our parts!"

A hurricane was forecast to be in the area sometime in the evening. Forecasters were convinced that it would just be a tropical storm with a lot of rain when it arrived in the Middle Town area. The outside grey skies indicated it would arrive on schedule.

Fortunately, one of the men was the designated driver for the crew. He gathered his alcohol soaked buddies and they made their way to their truck Dinato followed them back to The School. The driver got out of the truck. Dinato noticed that the other two had found sleeping space in the back of their truck and were snoring contentedly.

The driver assured him that he could complete the job by himself and asked Dinato not to call the company. Dinato could not bring himself to be the cause of two men losing their jobs, so he watched as the driver pulled on his tool belt and set off to complete the re-keying job. A few sprinkles of rain dotted his windshield as he called Brian Witaker to let him know that the lock company was back on the job.

Chapter Seven

The foreign language teachers, Albert Sanchez and the Jesuit Latin teacher, were laughing at something Sanchez had said in Spanish. Witaker knew it was something obscene, Sanchez seldom did anything that wasn't when speaking to or about adults.

Witaker took a telephone call from Pete Dinato as the two sat in front of his desk. He was relieved that the lock people were back and should finish before 5 PM.

Sanchez had purchased commercial Arabic software that would work in the language lab. It was a "hear and say" type of program. No Arabic language was offered and Sanchez wanted to have something available should any adult or student want to begin to learn it. It was an admirable initiative and Witaker had given his support to the purchase.

Sanchez and the Jesuit had been curious enough to listen to the program for about 30 minutes and both had a different take on what was being said. Sanchez had taken great interest in the virgins Allah promised and the Jesuit proclaimed that there was only one Virgin. They wanted Witaker to determine if the software was appropriate when each of them had questions about the content. Witaker told them to bring the software to his office. Arabic and Chinese were on hold.

An angry June Prior entered as the Jesuit and Sanchez left. The Make-Up class she had initiated this year was designed to assist young ladies in the proper use of face coatings.

The class list for Make-Up included three boys. Although all elective classes were open to both sexes, students usually stayed away from those that might make them subject to ridicule if they took them. However, the three boys had the support of each other and enrolled in the course. She wanted them out.

Two of the boys were wide receivers on the football team and wanted detailed instructions on how to apply eye black under their eyes. The entrepreneurial third boy did small magic tricks for birthday parties and wanted to expand his business to include a clown. He wanted instructions on applying clown face creams. The teacher knew nothing about either of them. Further, having the boys in the class would inhibit the girls, make them nervous and create a possible injury as they plucked their eyebrows. Besides, she continued, she had planned on having a lesson on bikini waxing and that lesson would have to be cancelled.

Mr. Witaker calmed the lady and told her he would contact their guidance counselors to see if another elective might be more appropriate for them. He asked her to adjust the maximum class size in the Course Selection booklet to three less than she had on her class list. The guidance staff had an overload excuse to reassign the boys.

As the home economics teacher left, Witaker made a note to contact the nurse to see if bikini waxing could be dangerous.

Brian Witaker had the task of meeting with Mr. Wiles. He had Slice set a meeting with him before he left.

The line at his door was gone. He had time for an afternoon coffee break.

Chapter Eight

On the football field Coach DeBishop was running the afternoon practice. Though the conditioning of the players was good, they weren't. The team was young and small. They had no experience at most positions except center and he had trouble snapping the ball to young JD. The timid quarterback just wanted to move away as quickly as possible and when the ball was snapped, he often had retreated leaving the ball in the center's crotch. Thinking the ball exchange had been made, the center sprung from his stance to complete his blocking assignment not knowing the ball lay on the ground.

Repeated running of the plays found a loose ball on the ground more often than not. The frustrated coach had been forced to redesign the assignment of the fullback so that he no longer did any blocking or ball carrying. The fullback's new assignment was to recover fumbles made in the exchange of the ball from the center to the quarterback.

Homeless Joe always watched the practices and saw the continued mistakes. Having spent many days at the horse racing track he had an idea. In his roaming of the school and avoiding Billy Evans at night, Joe found and old pair of yellow football shoes. He cut them into two patches and attached them to a headset. The result was a set of blinders much as timid horses wear when racing. When placed on the head with the headset over the ears and the blinders blocking any side distractions, it might help the young QB to at least get the ball from the center. Also, he would not be able to hear the threats from opposing linebackers.

Homeless Joe approached Coach DeBishop from downwind so as not to let his smell ruin the meeting. He explained the device in detail. The coach looked at what he had been given and thought it worth a try.

Coach DeBishop gave the device to the young quarterback before practice. He made sure that the meeting was in his office so as not to embarrass the young man. JD got a larger helmet and put the device on under it. The smell of the old shoes didn't seem a bother, nor did the device. He agreed to wear it in practice.

While JD made the helmet exchange in his office, DeBishop had talked to the team explaining what the QB would be wearing. He asked them not to laugh, just to practice as if nothing had changed. With the extra large helmet and yellow blinders, JD looked like a yellow taxi with both back doors open. But he had gotten a whole lot better, less timid and gained more confidence with each play. The fumbles had disappeared and JD was becoming good at what he needed to do.

Coach DeBishop knew the boy couldn't wear the device in a game but the kid would wear it long enough to gain game confidence...he hoped! However, he knew he was in for some trouble when JD's father found out that his son was practicing with the device and looking like some nag approaching the starting gate at a cheap claiming race. The word would get out tonight and the coach would deal with it tomorrow.

Meanwhile the lad had just completed his first pass. The two assistant coaches ran and hugged the boy. One yelled, "This horse is a stallion, not some friggin' mare! Now, just remember to take a crap as you leave the stable so you'll be at your best going down the stretch." The boy didn't hear him and the rest of the squad didn't understand what had been said.

DeBishop winced and gave the next play using his fingers so that JD could give it in the huddle.

The coach turned and found Homeless Joe in the grey gloom of the afternoon and gave him a wave and thumbs up. Joe returned the gesture and moved back to The School hoping to get more of those cookies from the Doggy Shaped cookie jar when the staff cleared the area.

Chapter Nine

On an adjacent field the soccer team went through their drills. Coach Santos had a loaded team. He had talked to Mrs. Thiesman and knew the team would be disappointed when they found out that the nude model would have her privates covered with something from the Gap. He was looking for just a little edge in the conference championship game and the model would have been just the ticket.

Carlos had come to Memorial High School directly from Brazil and had a green card! Standing only 5'2", the boy was amazing. He could head the ball better than most players could kick it. He could hook or slice corner kicks into the goal. The 15 year-old sophomore was the best player Santos ever had.

However, the rest of the team didn't trust him. The boy spoke no English but Santos was able to communicate with him in the little Portuguese he knew. The two-way chatter left the other boys wondering what was being said. Santos' team suffered from paranoia and they blamed it on the "foreigner."

At the annual Our Lady of Fatima festivities at the Portuguese Club, Coach Santos had his picture in the paper with his young star player. They were smiling and had pastry crumbs on their face. The newspaper headline read, "COACH AND STAR PLAYER READY TO FEAST ON OPPONENTS."

As the practice went on, Santos knew he had problems. No one would pass the ball to the new player. Further the team called him "Gay Carlos." He had not even been in school to register for the nude art class, but that didn't matter to the team. He was the only one not in the class and, therefore, he was gay.

Coach Santos took off his hat and called the team together. He spoke for 15 minutes to the team explaining the need for team work and the acceptance of the young star. Carlos just smiled and stared at the coach, he didn't understand one word. The talk seemed to be working until Santos heard one player whisper to another, "See, the foreigner is giving coach the eye. He wants to make it with him."

Santos exploded and yelled at the team in a combination of English and Portuguese. Thus half of what he said fell on confused ears. Finally, the coach calmed and let the team know that anyone calling anyone names would be dismissed from the team. Also, he told them that unless they could work as a team, he would dismiss all of them and use the junior varsity for games. He waved them away and the shocked boys ran back to the gymnasium. Several were seen patting Carlos on the back.

It still was going to be a difficult coaching year. The first game was in three days and he had to get Carlos a girlfriend.

Chapter Ten

The band was practicing in the parking lot under the grey skies. The entire paved areas of the school had been swept earlier in the week and all surface markings repainted. The assembled group of musicians looked like any group of kids their age during the summer. Most wore shorts and many had flip flop clad feet. The rag tag group was loosely aligned as they stood, some tuning their instruments as they chatted with each other.

Band Director, Mark Phillips, took care of the music part of the band. Fifty year-old retired Marine gunnery sergeant Sam Popham was teaching them to march. It was the sergeant's first time teaching marching to high school students. He needed a few extra coins to get the military channel on his Direct TV, so he had taken the job.

Phillips had given the band three Sousa pieces and they were not bad in playing them standing still. But marching and playing didn't seem to fit his band. They were musically out of sync once the sergeant gave the first "Left, Right…"

Patience wasn't in the sergeant's nature. The decorated Marine asked them to put down their instruments. It took a few minutes until he had them re-aligned and he took them into a straight forward march. Nothing hard, just left, right, etc. They stepped on each other's heals and stumbled as someone stepped on the back of a flip flop. The gunny sergeant gave a "Band Halt!" He knew how to handle this situation.

The Gunny realigned them and began, "All right, you piss ants. Every time you get out of step I'm going to kick your ass. Makes no never mind if you got nuts or not, your ass is getting my boot. If your god damn parents and this friggin' school didn't teach you left from right, this old gunny sergeant will!"

He continued, "If you can't learn to march while you're carrying instruments, you'll stumble and drive a clarinet through your empty skull or roll with a tuba down into the crick. You are going to march on a football field with markers every ten yards and if you can count and know your left from right, good shit is going to happen. Do you all get my drift?"

Phillips had not worked with Popham before and he wasn't about to mess with his methods if they were successful, nor was he about to mess with the gunny himself.

The students stood tall, most frightened by the sergeant and his outburst. He certainly had their attention while they stood at attention. Fear can be a great motivator and the gunny had in-stilled that in the young people.

The sergeant looked at the nice lines that had now formed and said, "Now take off those Jesus shoes you call flip flops and feel the pain of the pavement. When I say 'Left', I want to hear 60 left flat feet slapping pavement. Fear my boot, young people, THINK before you step. Let's get this god damn mess of cow dung moving forward!"

In the grey afternoon 60 band members moved in unison, their bare feet making a solitary sound as they moved away from the pile of shoes and instruments. Within 20 minutes the band was marching well enough for the sergeant to stop them. They competently did a left face on command and waited in-structions.

The gunny stood before them. He had a slight smile on his face, as did band director Phillips. The sergeant told them, "Now get your footwear and those brass things you call in-struments. We'll see if we got something here if no one does a pole vault on a trombone or something. Let's see if you piss ants can play while walking."

Phillips took his place in front of the band while the sergeant moved to the side.

Phillips gave the signal to begin playing as the band marched in unison toward the football field. The drums rolled and the sound of *Stars and Stripes Forever* filled the grey air as they grew smaller in the afternoon light.

The band passed by the lock company truck. The drums and music didn't even disturb the drunken snoring men sleeping in the rear. Gunny sergeant Popham saw the drunks and heard their snoring and figured that they should be standing at attention as the band played the standard marching song for military parades. He muttered, "Unpatriotic bastards," as he and the band passed by.

Chapter Eleven

Brain Witaker had a few minutes before Mr. Wiles was to meet with him. Witaker had also requested the attendance of the union rep at the meeting. He wanted to be sure that no second hand information came from what could be a potential problem from the dismissal of the man.

When his office had been re-keyed, Witaker also had a new lock on a cabinet hidden behind his professional books in what appeared to be a wooden bookcase. He had emptied the cabinet before it was re-keyed. He didn't want anyone to know that the cabinet contained a 9MM Glock hand gun and 6 clips of ammunition.

After Columbine and other invasions of high schools Witaker had decided that if he became a building principal, someone or several people in the building should be armed. He and the five men with military service backgrounds all were packing heat and had a plan to combat any intruders if it came to pass. Someone had to defend the people in the building and they were the chosen ones.

During his first summer of being principal of The School, Witaker met with the five ex-servicemen, Bill Soden ex-Navy, George DeWalt ex-paratrooper, Hank Desmond, ex- Army, Samual Johansen ex-Navy seal, and Dingo Walters ex-Air

Force, and they had all agreed to the plan. Hidden cabinets were built into each classroom where the men taught. Each purchased similar weapons and had applied and received a gun permit from the local police. So as not to bring attention to the application for gun permits, they submitted them at intervals and took weapons classes at different times. No one suspected that six armed men would be in the building to meet any intruders.

The six men met monthly at a private pistol range each month. They were proficient with their weapons and serious about their cause. However, what they were doing was a direct violation of Board of Education policy and probably violated local, state, and federal laws as well. No matter, no one was going to shoot up their people without retaliation. They were not going to wait for some slow SWAT team to come into the building to clean up dead bodies.

Their plan was simple. Whenever The School went into a Code Red lockdown, they unlocked the gun cabinets, locked the students in the rooms, and went into the hallway. Each was strategically located in the building and had an assigned area of armed responsibility.

They had run a drill the week before school opened and the response was military and organized. In less than two minutes, each man was in position and communicating via walkie talkies with each other, with Witaker assuming the command of the operation.

No one was to open fire unless fired upon or if the intruder began firing upon any individual in the building. The six gunslingers were well trained and ready to combat anyone meaning grievous harm to their territory. Their code of silence about their operation included not telling their families. They would find out only if the six drew second blood.

Witaker wanted to meet with the security staff to reinforce his concern for their past behavior in dealing with students. He also wanted them to greet the new female staff member in a gentlemanly manner and acquaint her with procedures, the students, and the red zones within the building.

The red zones were the areas that were the most vulnerable to student misbehavior. These included alcoves, stairways, under stairways, and around any room where a substitute teacher might be assigned. Security also was allowed casual walk throughs of the boys' lavatories just as a cautious presence. The new female staff member would be an asset to the security of the girl's use of the lavatories.

Witaker had Slice set-up a meeting with the security staff after the meeting with Mr. Wiles. He also included the Dean and the assistants to the meeting. Administration had to be on the same page regarding student discipline and this would afford them the opportunity to do so.

He looked from his desk to see Mrs. Petrone, the union rep, and Mr. Wiles awaiting his attention outside his office.

Chapter Twelve

Brian Witaker closed the door to his office. Mrs. Petrone opened a note pad, took out a pen and was ready to take notes on the meeting. She knew of the problems Mr. Wiles was having and felt sorry for the man. She knew him as a good teacher and a quiet colleague.

Mr. Wiles sat in front of the desk. It was his second time in the office that day and he knew the meeting was not to be a good one. He squirmed as he arranged himself. He couldn't bring himself to make eye contact with Mr. Witaker or Mrs. Petrone.

Witaker began by praising all the good work Mr. Wiles had done in the past. His evaluations showed him to be a fine teacher who had established a reputation for creative assignments. His leaf collection project in which students gathered leaves from as many trees as possible in the area and identifying each of them had won recognition from the state association of science teachers.

As Mrs. Petrone took notes, Witaker revisited the problems Mr. Wiles had last year with the hole drilled into the female lavatory. He explained, step by step, what they had agreed upon to assist Mr. Wiles address his problem. Despite visitations to a psychiatrist and the meetings with the school psychologist, Witaker told them, the problem remained. He explained that Mr. Wiles had requested a portable drill from the maintenance crew and that Pete Dinato had seen him going to the closet adjacent to the female lavatory.

Witaker told Mrs. Petrone and Mr. Wiles that he directed Mr. Jiminez to check on the closet and that Moon Pie had found a freshly drilled hole through the concrete blocks from the closet into the lavatory. Moon Pie had taken the initiative to casually walk into Mr. Wiles' room and noted concrete dust on his shoes.

Witaker asked Mr. Wiles to respond as a shocked Mrs. Petrone continued taking notes. Mr. Wiles nervously waved his hand and apologized. He knew it was a weak response, but it was the best he could do. Mr. Witaker had been more than fair with him and Wiles knew that he wanted him to succeed. He just couldn't overcome his urges.

A long pause followed. Brian Witaker chose his words carefully and said, "Mr. Wiles, I am truly sorry to have to do and say this. You are a good man and a talented teacher. However, I can not condone your behavior and have a responsibility to protect the privacy implied in the use of the lavatories. I reluctantly must ask for your resignation. Should you refuse to resign I will be forced to bring your name and circumstances before the Superintendent and the Board of Education for moral turpitude. You will have competent attorneys to represent you, but I am certain that we have enough evidence to present a strong case for your dismissal. Because school opens tomorrow, I am relieving you of your teaching responsibilities as of right now and will recommend a paid suspension if you chose to argue my decision."

Witaker continued, "Should you lose your case in a formal hearing with the Board of Education, you will lose your certification and your name will be in the news. Should you win, and I don't think you will, your name will carry the taint of the hearing. Either way, it has been my observation of similar cases, that your career will be over."

Mr. Wiles had tears coming from his eyes. Mrs. Petrone paused and the creases in her forehead revealed her pain as well. Wiles hung his head so that Witaker couldn't see him crying.

The lump in Brian Witaker's throat and the gastric juices invading his stomach wall did not deter him from his deeply sad duty. He continued. "If you resign I will not give you a recommendation for employment in another school district but will not recommend the withdrawal of your teaching certificate. If you get professional help to overcome your problem and a psychiatrist certifies that you are well enough to continue in the teaching profession, you may be able to return as a viable and able teacher in another town or state."

With the glimmer of hope extended to him, Mr. Wiles raised his head. Mrs. Petrone was writing furiously as Mr. Witaker paused and waited until the union rep caught up with her notes before continuing. "Whatever you choose to do, you must do it now. If you resign for personal reasons beginning today, I will forward it immediately to the Superintendent. If you choose to argue the charges against you, I will recommend to the Superintendent that you be placed on paid leave until a hearing date is set. Either way you will not be coming to school tomorrow. You must clear your room of all your personal items before 6 PM and leave your keys with me. I will need to inspect your room and any items that you are taking. Your computer was shut down ten minutes ago and the computer technician is now in your room downloading any material that has your name on it. He will give it to you before you leave. The head of security will be with you when you leave my office, remain with you as you put your personal items together, and return with you to my office before you leave."

Mr. Wiles sat and took it all in. Mrs. Petrone had stopped taking notes and her furrowed face and brow had turned into a gentle and caring look. She felt for the man and understood that Witaker had given him ample opportunity to succeed. The sad and serious meeting had drained her as well.

Brian Witaker's face had softened and his stomach had stopped churning. He continued, "You may want to consult with Mrs. Petrone before you make your decision. But you must make it now. If you want, I'll leave so you can talk with her."

Mr. Wiles thought as Brain Witaker rose to leave. His eyes had dried and he calmly responded, "I have no need to consult, my resignation will be immediate. If you will give me some paper and a pen, I will do so right now."

Mrs. Petrone rose and hugged Mr. Wiles, turned and left the office as he wrote his resignation letter and signed it.

He handed the letter to Brian Witaker and said, "I am sorry for all that I did to cause you so much distress. I want you to know that I appreciate all that you have tried to do for me. I will make every effort to restore my good name. Thank you, sir."

Mr. Witaker reached out and shook Wiles' hand. The meeting was over and both were relieved with the results. Somehow Witaker felt that Mr. Wiles would succeed and hoped for the opportunity to give him a recommendation for a teaching position at some future time. Good teachers are hard to find, he thought, and Wiles still had much to offer to the young people in some other high school.

The head of security met Wiles at the door and they moved slowly out of the office. Brian Witaker cursed his job. He felt that his vision of helping others and been detoured by the meeting.

Chapter Thirteen

Mr. Witaker had forgotten that he needed to talk to the young music teacher and phoned the music room to have him come to the office. The young enthusiastic fellow had to be told to stop his gyrations and hip thrusts during his Music of the 60's class.

Mark Phillips answered the phone. The band director expressed his concerns about gunny sergeant Popham's use of language during the just ended marching band practice. Gunny was still on the property and Witaker had him paged on the all-call.

Almost verbatim, Phillips gave Witaker the language the gunny had used. The band director also explained that the crusty old Marine had gotten positive results and that the band performed at the highest level since Phillips had been there. But they both knew that once the students reached home the telephone would be ringing.

The young music teacher arrived before the sergeant. Witaker gently told him that he needed to temper his enthusiasm to the rock sounds as they played in class. Witaker also suggested that he get his pants one size larger because the students were prone to talk about his "package" upon leaving the class. The young man blushed and thanked Witaker for giving

81

him the message. He would try to be less demonstrative during the class and would get a new tailor that would make better use of trouser space.

Gunny sergeant Popham had come highly recommended by the superintendent and had been hired by the central office. He was a legend in the community and led the annual parades clad in full dress uniform with a chest full of medals including a silver and bronze stars. He had two purple hearts and still had the vigor of a much younger man.

Witaker had interviewed him and liked him immediately. The fact that he had no experience working with school aged students was a concern, but Witaker had taken a chance.

The sergeant entered and stood front and center in front of the principal's desk

"I know why you want to see me," the sergeant said. "I believe that I may have scared some of the kids and you are about to hear from a bunch of pissed off parents."

"Sir," he continued, "I will sit outside by the telephone and apologize to every single one of them for my language and actions. But I will not apologize for teaching them to march forward, backward, oblique, and to follow directions to each command. Nor will I apologize for any missed notes while they were playing."

Witaker smiled. He knew the sergeant wouldn't run away from his mistakes. This brave man could take the flack from anyone and do it with grace and courage. Witaker also knew that any parent who called and talked with the gunny would be in awe just having him on the phone. But he needed a lesson in working with young people.

"Gunny," Witaker said, "you had before you some kids who can't even drive yet. Band students come from homes in which parents do not swear in front of them. Sure, most of them have heard swear words before, but never from an adult in authority. You owe them an apology as well. And if you ever use that kind of language again in this school or on the school grounds, I'll personally snatch every hair from your ass with barbeque tongs!"

The gunny sergeant gave a smile. Witaker was talking a language he could understand clearly. He responded, "Yes, Sir! Now, if you'll provide me with a list of band students and their telephone numbers, I'll call every one and apologize to them and their parents."

"But," the sergeant continued, "you should have seen them little sumbitches march, Mr. Witaker! They aren't going to be half bad after the old gunny gets them on the football field wearing softer shoes and using better words from this old pie hole. It won't happen again."

The sergeant stood at attention until Slice brought in the band list. She guided him to an empty desk and he began dialing.

Chapter Fourteen

It was nearing late afternoon when the female lavatory custodian knocked at Brian

Witaker's door. Witaker seldom saw the lady. It was alleged that she spent a good time of her day sleeping a stall in the largest female lavatory. That she and Billy Evans disliked one another was obvious.

Evans had tried to have a letter of reprimand placed in her file. It was based on no facts, just Evans trying to get rid of her using Witaker as the agent. Evans was the one who suffered because of the attempt as Witaker had written a letter of reprimand about him for his mean effort to put a blemish on her record. Evans didn't blame Witaker, he blamed "Sleeping Beauty" and did everything he could as her superior to make it uncomfortable for her. That she spent most of her time in the female lavatory was her way of avoiding him.

She related to Mr.Witaker that Billy Evans had pushed an AV cart with a TV/VCR into her supply closet and left it there. She didn't know why but she suspected something.

Witaker thanked her and made his way to the supply closet. The AV cart was pushed against the wall. Leading from the VCR was a fiber optic wire that led into the wall. Witaker knew that the only room in the building that had fiber optic cabling was the media center and the supply closet wall where the AV cart was left led into the media center.

Growing very suspicious, Witaker called one of the security personnel and met him in the media center. A large screen TV was installed on the wall opposite the supply closet. The security man got on a chair and loosened one of the ceiling tiles. A fiber optic wire led from the supply room and was connected to the media center TV.

It all came together for Witaker. Evans had connected the misplaced AV cart into the supply closet and attached it to the media center TV. He also knew that Evans had requested a media center schedule. Evans planned something bad. But what?

He returned to the office and called in the head of security. They brainstormed for a few minutes. The head of security had an idea and asked Mr. Witaker for his phone book.

The security head called the local adult video store. Billy Evans had been in yesterday and rented a XXX movie and was to return it at the end of the week.

Billy Evans was going to play a XXX movie into the media center during a class and blame it on the female custodian! At the same time, he would break the "no frolicking" record of the media center. Two security men returned to the supply closet and found the tape hidden in a big box of sanitary napkins. It was time for Billy Evans to go.

Chapter Fifteen

After receiving the XXX video tape from the security people, Witaker reminded them that a new female member of their staff was arriving tomorrow. He told them to treat her as a lady and take the responsibility of teaching her the school policies and procedures.

Knowing of the demise of Mr. Wiles and seeing Mr. Witaker's temper regarding the Billy Evans fiasco, the men took his words seriously. There would be no problems accepting the new member in the morning. He directed them to locate Billy Evans in the building and to bring him to the office. They were not to tell him what it was about and Evans was not to go anywhere except directly to Witaker's office and wait until he was summoned. The security men were to wait with him.

Witaker used the all-call to get Moon Pie Jimonez to the office. Jimonez was the building union steward and Witaker wanted him in attendance during the meeting with Evans. When a puzzled Jimonez arrivived, Witker called in Billy Evans. This meeting was going to be far easier than the Wiles dismissal.

Evans and Jimonez sat. Witaker pulled out Evans personnel file and began, "I have strong evidence," he said as he held up the XXX video tape, "that you were planning on playing this into media center while a class was in session. The adult video store has confirmed that you rented it and it contains the same serial rental number. You placed an AV cart in the female custodian supply closet and wired the VCR to the media center."

Witaker looked directly at Evans and said, "While the evidence is circumstantial, it plus all of your past documented behavior, is enough for me to immediately place you on a paid suspension. I have contacted the Superintendent and he has agreed with the recommendation for the suspension." The two shocked men were speechless as Witaker continued, "Place your key ring on my desk."

Evans took the key ring from his belt loop and gave it to Witaker. Witaker stood and said, "You will now be escorted out of the building by security personnel. While on suspension, you are not to enter the building nor are you to be on school grounds. You will be arrested if you do so. You may make arrangements with the head of security to come back to retrieve any personal items you may have. Also, you will have to pay any late fees for the video rental because it will be held until after your suspension hearing."

The two security men came into the office at Witaker's beckon. He told them, "Take Mr. Evans out of the building and make sure he leaves the school grounds. He is not to re-enter the building and should you see him in or around the school, you are to immediately contact me. Mr. Evans has been suspended and all here are to treat this in a confidential manner."

Before they left the office, Witaker completed the suspension task. He said to Evans, "You will be contacted by central office notifying you of a hearing date. All questions and phone calls will go through them. Do not call here."

Evans and the two security men left and he heard the front door close behind them. Witaker turned to Jimonez and directed him to give the key ring to the senior night custodian who was temporarily going the replace Evans. Witaker had talked to the night man explaining that Evans wouldn't be around for a while and that he was to fill in for him. Witaker would give him further information tomorrow morning.

While the Evans suspension meeting was going on, the sober lock company man had entered the main office. He waved and shook a key ring with the new master keys in the air catching Mr. Witaker's attention. The lock company man left the keys on the counter in the main office, waved again and left.

Chapter Sixteen

Mr. Jimonez left with Evans' key ring. Sleeping Beauty was getting ready to leave. She was well rested. No bells were ringing today and her only chore had been to give Mr. Witaker a heads-up on Billy Evans. Her butt was a little sore from sitting on a toilet seat for so long. She had worked most of the summer in the cleaning of the building. She needed to get back into "sitting shape" for the long school year.

She saw Mr. Jimonez walking down the hallway. It wasn't his cleaning area and he seldom left his assigned space. Rubbing her sore butt she yelled, "Hey, Moon Pie, what are you doing up here?"

He answered, "Well, Billy Evans just got his ass thrown out of the building and two security guys gave him the toss. I'm bringing his keys to the Ralph, the night guy. Ralph's going to be the honcho for a while."

The female custodian withheld her gas. She had eaten too many cookies from that doggy shaped cookie jar she had thrown away from Ms. Aphros' room. She had seen Moon Pie bringing it back down the hall that afternoon and wondered what that was all about.

She didn't ask why Evans had been escorted out. She was so happy that he was gone that she had to expel her gas. Waving her hand behind her sore butt to move the odor down the hall, she yelled, "They finally got that son-of-bitch!"

Mr. Jimonez gave her a weird look and made his way through the polluted air. That is one strange lady, he thought.

Passing by the science rooms, Moon Pie checked to see if the doggy shaped cookie jar was where he had placed it. There it was between the two skeleton skulls on the shelf, just as Mr. Witaker had told him to do.

He met Ralph, the night man, in the locker alcove and gave him Evans' key ring.

Ralph had been working in The School since it opened. He was a good cleaner, kept his distance and did his job. He liked working nights. He was a little hurt when Evans had received the head custodian position, but never complained. He was a good man who could be trusted.

Ralph thanked Jimonez, put away his cleaning cart and made his way to the main custodial room. He wouldn't start his new responsibilities until mid-morning tomorrow but he wanted to get a feel for the space that Evans inhabited.

Ralph was always the last one out of the building each night. He set the alarm and made sure that all the night and emergency lights were working. A half hour before setting the alarm, he always left the rear parking lot door ajar. When he came back it would be closed. He knew that Homeless Joe was safe somewhere inside the building.

Billy Evans never bothered him in his nightly tasks. Evans was usually doing laps, tucked in for the night, or sucking hemp while watching porno.

Evans had changed the lock on the head custodian's room. Not knowing, the lock company had done as Evans requested, and gave him the only key to his room. He had put it in his pocket earlier in the day.

Ralph tried every key on the ring. None opened the door. Using his walkie talkie, Ralph called Mr. Witaker and told him about the situation. Witaker told him to get a crow bar and break into the room.

Ralph found a crow bar in the cafeteria store room. After several attempts he got into Billy Evans sanctuary. What Ralph found overwhelmed him. Plush wall-to-wall carpeting, the same found in the principal's office, covered the concrete floor. The carpeting had been installed five years when JD. Wilson was the principal. The same paneling covering the walls in the principal's office stretched across two walls.The paneling had been put up, again five years ago, when the office was redecorated.

A large screen TV was situated on one wall and an oak recessed book case on another. The TV was similar to the one in the media center, as was the book case. A recliner was situated in front of the TV. It was the same kind of recliner found in the health suite which was used for blood drives. What was supposed to be a tool bin, instead held a hospital bed, a night stand and a dresser. The bed and the stand were similar to ones used in the health suite The dresser looked like the one that had been listed as missing from the home economics room. An air-conditioning duct fed cool air into the suite. Evans had apparently tapped into the main office air-conditioning duct and had a constant cool flow of conditioned air.

It appeared that Billy Evans had either taken each item in the suite from somewhere in the building or convinced a contractor that the head custodian's room was part of their job order. The conniving man had created a masterpiece, a living area far better than any of the staff had in their homes!

Billy Evans had taken advantage of the timid condition of JD Wilson. Evans didn't miss any opportunity to get in on re-decorating or adding something to a purchase order. He also had taken furniture from other rooms in The School. He was responsible for conducting a search for the missing items and declared them lost or stolen. In fact, the items were safely locked away in his suite. They were not missing or stolen, just relocated into Evans' suite.

Ralph called Mr. Witaker again and reported what he had found in the custodial room.

Witaker was not surprised by the report Ralph gave to him. Witaker called security and directed them to bring a video recorder and camera with them and to video tape and to photograph the entire suite. The suspension was about to become a formal dismissal hearing.

When security arrived with the cameras, Ralph uttered a phrase his father used when amazed by something. "Jesus to Jesus, General Jackson, and ten great men of America, that Billy Evans was really something!"

Chapter Seventeen

The School had almost emptied as Brian Witaker finished his notes on the two dismissal meetings. The dean and the assistant principals had come in to talk about any problems they had encountered.

The teacher scheduling snafus had been corrected or explained. The master schedule was a good one and the computer easily allowed for minor adjustments to it. The names of the teachers taking the places of Ms. Ledbetter and Mr. Wiles had been inputted. The accompanying student schedules with the name adjustments had been printed. Stacks of student schedules lined the office counter awaiting teacher pick-up in the morning.

An unhappy Ms. Aphros had taken her missing cookie jar problem to the dean who had known absolutely nothing about it. The dean and Ms. Aphros had only one connection; they both loved dogs and spoke about them on occasion. Ms. Aphros felt that the dean would better understand her grief better than Witaker. But the dean was a black lab guy and disliked any dog not large enough to hump on your knee. However, the dean conjured enough sympathy to calm her.

Witaker gave them the details of the Mr. Wiles resignation and the Billy Evans suspension. None seemed surprised by either. They didn't quite understand why Ms. Ledbetter had left, but took it for granted that Mr. Witaker had done everything to help her. It had been a long day for the administrators and they had families awaiting them.

When the dean and assistants left, only Brian Witaker, Ralph, and two other custodians were in The School. As usual on a non-school day, the other two custodians punched out at 6 PM. The end of Ralph's shift was 9 PM.

It had started to rain and the winds escalated enough to hear an occasional rattle of the front door. The forecasters were accurate as far as the arrival of the rain shield of the approaching hurricane. Computer projections indicated that Middle Town would be on the safe side of it, thus producing winds that would not cause heavy damage.

Brian Witaker sat back in his chair, put his feet on his desk and locked his fingers behind his head. He was tired. Both the morning staff meeting and the Teaching Techniques presentation had drained a lot of his energy. He was hungry and wanted to get home to see his family. At times during the day, they seemed to be the only sane side of his life.

It was not uncommon for Witaker to spend 12 – 14 hours in The School, but those occurred during the school year when evening events dictated his attendance. Now he wanted to get home to make sure that his house was ready for some high winds and heavy rain. His leaving would have to wait a little longer; he needed to reflect on the day in the quiet of his office.

His staff had decreased since the morning. Ms. Ledbetter, Mr. Wiles, and the head custodian were gone. He hoped he never saw Ms. Ledbetter again, she just seemed to collapse after her engagement had been broken. In his mind he wished her well, but had a feeling that he would hear her name in the near future from some attorney representing her.

The worst experience a principal can have is to dismiss a teacher. When something goes awry with another human being, it is a tragedy. The loss of Mr. Wiles was such an event. Witaker truly hoped the man would get help to salvage his good name and career. Witaker made a mental note to call him in several months to check on him.

Getting Billy Evans out the door was not such a tragic event. Evans' full personnel folder was overflowing with documentation of his conniving behavior. Witaker felt sure that Evans would never set foot in the building again. Security had packed his personal items and they would be delivered to his parent's house.

All the problems presented to him during the day had been solved or were solvable. The recently vacated teaching positions were filled and central office had honored his request for two more permanent substitutes. Only one item kept running through his mind. What had happened to the doggy shaped cookie jar that Moon Pie was supposed to have taken back to Ms. Aphros' room? Jimonez had left before he could question him as to where he had placed it.

As far as he could determine, The School was ready for opening day. The hurricane had been down-graded to a tropical storm and all indications were that it would not create any delay in the opening of the Middle Town Schools.

Brian Witaker's day was over. He was ready for the new school year.

Chapter Eighteen

Billy Evans was sitting on a stool at Larry's Sports Bar. His appearance was unusual, he seldom came into the place except to place an occasional bet on a football or basketball game. He always lost because he was a hunch player.

Seated at the bar, Shotsy Ritalli, bookie Patsy LeBeau, and former policeman Ace Rickets were throwing down Fleishman shots and beer chasers. Their butts hung over the stools like tires on a wheel rim. Shotsy and Ace wore stained golf shirts that barely encompassed their beer bellies. Patsy had on a hunting jacket with pockets in which he carried his betting slips.

They were regulars, each had their own stool with Shotsy having the one closest to the men's room because his bladder and prostate made for frequent trips to the foul smelling lavatory. Shotsy went so often that he left his fly unzipped which saved a few seconds in his return to his stool.

Larry, the bartender and owner of the place, only had two rules for the bar. All fights must be taken outside and no urinating in the old telephone booth in the back. For most of the day he read the paper, racing forms, and tabloids. His conversation with the regulars was limited to one syllable comments between pouring shots of the low grade whiskey and drawing beer from the tap.

Only Shotsy had attended The School. His high school days ended when he goosed an English teacher when she bent over to help the student in front of him.

Larry and Patsy had more education. They had gotten to their junior years in a high school nearby that had taken Middle Town students on a tuition basis. Both were worldly, but lacked the attention to go further in an academic setting. Patsy could do math in his head, but the x stuff in algebra made no sense to him. He already was running numbers and making more than his teachers. Ace had graduated from a nearby high school and had attended the police academy. Thus, he was considered the scholar of the group.

Larry had inherited the bar from his father who had purchased it with his railroad retirement money. He had worked in the bar since he had dropped out of school.

The bar did a good business. Three large screen TVs captured all the sports networks and the place was filled on nights when the Red Sox, Yankees, or Mets were playing. Football Saturdays and Sundays also found the bar filled with men, some with their wives. The ladies were mostly beer drinkers. However, Larry's bar did stock cheap wines with screw top caps from which an occasional female might take a glass.

Shotsy, Patsy, Ace, and Larry had more than the bar in common. They all hated The School. The land on which it was built was a lot on which they played baseball as kids. They always voted against the education budget and rooted against any Beaver team and got angry when The School received any kind of accolade. It was a perfect place for Billy Evans to go with his misery.

The regulars were talking about the forthcoming hurricane and were angry that the TV kept interrupting their daily soap opera with updates on the location of the storm.

They had barely glanced up when Evans entered. Patsy was the first to see him and reached into a pocket of his hunting jacket for a pencil and a betting slip. Patsy thought to himself, here comes the money for my bar tab today.

Patsy figured he would only be in the bar for another half hour because Shotsy had started to eat pickled eggs. Shotsy would be ripe once the eggs got to the bottom of his huge stomach and Patsy wanted to get out before that happened. Larry always refused to sell pickled eggs to Shotsy because of the reaction in the nether regions of his bowels. But today, all the games were rained out, the crowd for tonight would be minimal, and Larry needed the egg income to cut his losses on the forecast of a small nightly assemblage.

Evans got their attention by throwing a twenty onto the bar and telling Larry to set up the bar for the others. He was now a friend for a while. Bars are like that.

The regulars listened to Evan's demise. Bar courtesy demands giving ear to the one who just bought the round. Amid the burps and ahs of shots being thrown down gullets, Evans gave his account of what had happened. He left out any details that might cast doubt on himself. The regulars listened until the shots and beers were drained and gradually looked back at the situation developing in the soap opera.

In the soap opera, Laura and Chad had just found out that DNA tests showed that Chad was not the father of their new baby. Apparently Laura had romped with another when Chad was away in Hollywood doing technical assistance on the screening of his script, *Dancing to Elevator Music*. Shotsy observed, "Why did they need a DNA test, the kid is black and they are as pale as Sam Adams ale?"

Evans redirected them by pushing forward a ten to refill their empties. He needed to reach them to get some salve for his injured ego.

Even Larry listened. He didn't like Evans because he had tried to buy pot from a local dealer in the bar one night and Larry would take no chances in his place being some drug den. As long as he was buying and not being obnoxious, Evans had earned his ear.

Ace could care less about Evans. He would drink when the bar filled up with shots and beer backers, but he disliked Evans. He knew that when he was the kid, Evans had filled his patrol car with restaurant garbage one Halloween night. Evans was a punk like everyone else between the ages of 13 and 18. But Ace listened because he wanted to know how badly someone had treated the a-hole. He hoped it included someone stomping on his groin or dropping a left hook to his jaw.

As Billy Evans told his side of the story he didn't know that the others were happy that he had been shit-canned. They couldn't even muster a frown at his story and knew a lie when they heard one.

Shotsy was able to throw in a "Too Bad." The others just nodded and waited for Evans to push forward the remainder of his money still sitting on the bar.

When the last of the bar money had been expended and his story ended, Evans waited for some feedback on his demise. None was forthcoming; the regulars had turned back to the soap opera. An irate Chad had just called Laura a harlot and was heading for the divorce lawyer. The nanny tried to quiet the crying child as Laura sobbed into the silk pillow on the divan. It was a much better story than the one they had just heard from Evans.

Shotsy had left to drain his tank. Patsy was counting his money stash from one of the hunting jacket pockets and calculating that it was about time for him to leave before Shotsy got really ripe. Larry was wiping the back of the bar, upset that Evans had only left a dime tip. Ace was thinking he should pull his stub nosed 38 so he could blow away Laura and put her out of her misery.

The TV channel was interrupted again by a weather update. The new forecast was met by a "sons a bitches" almost in unison from the regulars. In their minds, Evans had never been there.

Billy Evans left without a goodbye or thank you from the others. He was just another guy with a sad story and they had heard most of them.

As Evans left Ace commented, "Too had someone didn't do the Bristol stomp on his friggin'head." Shotsy nodded and gulped down another pickled egg as Patsy gathered himself to leave.

Larry mumbled and noted "Too bad, that school is better off without him. Hope another a-hole replaces him. A couple of guys were in earlier. They were fixing locks on the place and said it was some kind of zoo in there. No kids, just a bunch of overpaid teachers getting a free pass while sticking it up our asses and using our tax money for being there. Sons a bitches!"

Patsy and Ace left. Shotsy threw down another pickled egg with a beer chaser. No exiting remarks were exchanged. They would see each other when the bar opened in the morning. Tomorrow was a continuation of today, so why say good-bye?

Chapter Nineteen

As Brian Witaker reached to turn off his desk light to leave The School after his busy day, the telephone rang. It was the local newspaper wanting a comment on a boy named Harry Pearson. Witaker recognized the name. The boy had graduated last year, he was the one called "Harry Ass" who had mooned the TV security camera.

Harry Pearson had joined the Marines on graduation. The newspaper reporter told him that they had just found out that Harry Pearson had been killed in Iraq last week

His would be the first name on the Memorial High School brass plaque.

A saddened Brian Witaker told the reporter that Pearson had been an asset to the school and his community and that the news would shake the entire school. He was a well-liked boy who always gave his best. Witaker told the reporter that his heart went out to the young Marine's family

The reporter thanked him. Witaker hung his head in his hands. The stunning news changed several things. Witkaker also knew that he would treasure the video of Harry giving his last salute to The School. It was a young man's prank, an opportunity not ignored. It was not out of disrespect, just a young man daring enough to do it. Boys like Pearson would become men with whom Witaker could relate.

The high school prank would not hinder the young man from entering a good place in the great beyond. Witaker said a silent prayer, a tribute to refute that small misdemeanor if some heavenly spirit questioned it.

Brian Witaker went to the student record files from last year and pulled Harry Pearson's file. His mother Mary was a single parent. Guidance counselor notes showed that the Pearsons had moved into Middle Town when Harry was a freshman. His father Joseph, location unknown, had served in the Army and had trouble reconnecting upon his return and the mother was left to raise the boy herself.

Pearson had lettered in football for three years and had a modest academic record. A newspaper picture was enclosed. It showed an intense young football player wearing yellow shoes putting a devastating block on an opponent. Pearson had no serious discipline problems other than a few pranks. His application to the state university had placed him on the waiting list. The young man, it seemed, had entered the service with intentions of going to college after his discharge.

After returning the records to the file cabinet, Witaker stood at attention at his desk and began to plan for a school memorial service for the Marine. He reached into his desk and pulled out the security tape of the young man and placed it into the VCR. He turned on the TV and smiled as it played. When it ended, he saluted the TV monitor and turned off the TV/VCR.

Witaker looked out of his window and noticed a light on in the music room. He called and found that Mr. Phillips was still there. He asked Philips for a special favor in the morning.

With slumped shoulders, Witaker turned out the lights and left the building. He was anxious to get home and hug his family.

Chapter Twenty

The 8 PM meeting of the Football Fathers was 20 minutes late in starting. The ever increasing winds and rain slowed down travel to the Eagles club. Just about all were in attendance. Each paranoid father wanted to protect his boy from a critical evaluation of their kid's performance and place on the team from the other fathers. Every father thought their boy should be a starter and that the boy selected to start ahead of their son was a "Peter Pan."

Most of the fathers showed up not to discuss ways of making money for the team. They came to criticize. Twenty-one of the men wanted to discuss fund raising events. The twenty-one had boys who had earned starting positions. One father had two sons starting and some men secretly called him a "greedy bastard."

The fifty fathers divided themselves along party lines. Even if their kid started, they sat with second and third team fathers who had the same party affiliation. Many of them still had bandages and visual bruises from the last brawling meeting.

They were meeting at the Eagles because the Elks had banned them from any future meetings. Someone had tried to hang another on the Elks' horns causing it to fall. One glass eye from the head had rolled away and was crushed by a father's work boot as he sucker punched another who was getting to his feet.

The barren room only had a cartoon of a past master feeding pigeons to a caged eagle. The bar was closed.

The chairman had no trouble getting order. The silence was heavy in the room as the fathers glared at each other. The door in the back of the room opened and Athletic Director, Joe Ritalli, came in. The fathers respected Joe, he was one of them. He also despised Coach DeBishop and had tried to undermine him every chance he got.

Joe was upset that the bar was closed. He needed a drink. A knowing father passed him a flask which he quickly drained.

The chairman simply acknowledged the AD and let him take over the meeting. No fund raising discussion would occur this rainy evening.

Joe began, "I don't care what friggin' party you guys belong to, we got problems." He nodded toward the timid quarterback's father, "DeBishop has your son wearing blinders and a headset. The kid looks like some alien."

There was a murmur from the gathering and disbelief on some faces. Joe went on, "I went into Witaker's office today to get some satisfaction and the guy sent me packing. You guys got to do something about those two before they screw up the entire season."

There was a louder murmur from the men and a lot of up and down head-shaking. The AD continued, "You guys got to stop knocking the crap out of each other. Think of DeBishop and Witaker as two tackling dummies and have at them hard. They need to be shown who is running that team and school. Dig in your toes and suck up your nuts and put some shoulders into those two dummies!"

The chairman thanked the AD for his attendance and Joe Ritalli left to find a bar open on his way home.

With one exception the group responded to the call for action. This evening would be devoted to finding ways to dump Witaker and DeBishop.

After adjournment, Moon Pie Jimonez, the only dissenter, called Brian Witaker and gave him the details of the meeting. Witaker thanked him, knowing he had time to meet the problem head on. He would deal with each father one on one. They were good men and would listen to the other side of every story if given the opportunity. The AD was another problem, but could be neutralized with some pressure from central office.

Moon Pie's son was just a kicker, but he would not be part of doing anything negative to the two men he knew and admired. He knew Mr. Witaker could handle anything this group threw at him, just as he did in sacking that snake, Billy Evans.

Chapter Twenty-One

With his windshield wipers at full speed, Brian Witaker pulled into the Memorial High School driveway at 6 AM. The heavy rain had begun at sunset last evening. The remnants of Hurricane Lowanda, now just a tropical depression, seemed to have settled right over the area. It was going to be a saturated day.

Witaker pulled into his parking place. Someone had taken the PRINCIPAL parking sign and replaced it with a soaked cardboard one which said "El Hombre."

As he exited his car, the strong odor of pig manure drifted from the neighboring farm. The old farmer must have had a delivery yesterday, just in time for the opening of school.

The storm drain in front of the bus loading area was flooded, leaving a large pool of water right in front of the covered patio entrance to the building. There were going to be a lot of wet feet stomping onto the newly waxed floors.

No lights could be seen in the building. With Billy Evans gone, the new head custodian had come from the night crew and he wasn't scheduled to begin until tomorrow.

Witaker noticed a bread delivery truck and a milk truck going around the driveway to the rear delivery door for the cafeteria. Evans usually opened that door at 6 AM so he didn't have to take the deliveries in by himself.

The extra police he had requested had been deployed to a flooded area in town. Walking around the flooded area, Witaker reached the front door. He put his master key into the newly re-keyed lock. It didn't work He tried several times without success.

He went to his car and took an umbrella from the trunk and trotted to the gym entrance. Again, the key did not open the door.

A very worried Witaker, ran to the swimming pool entrance and again was locked out. Running through the mud in his freshly shined shoes, he arrived at the cafeteria delivery entrance. The bread and milk men sat in their trucks awaiting the door opening.

Witaker waved to them and tried his master key in that lock with no success. He and everyone else had no access to the building!

Witaker told the delivery men to leave their deliveries at the door and they left while he tried calling the head of maintenance on his cell phone. After several attempts, he got a sleepy Pete Dinato on the line. Both confused men began to imagine the worst.

Dinato gave Witaker the telephone number of the lock company and said he would be at the high school as soon as possible. Witaker tried the number only to get a message that business hours were from 8 AM to 5 PM.

Returning to the front entrance, Witaker awaited the arrival of the maintenance head man.

The alarm system was activated and the vandal proof doors and windows were unbreakable. The heavy rain began to flood the entire parking area and the pig manure odor was trapped in the enclosed patio area.

Teachers began to arrive and gathered with Witaker on the patio. His explanation didn't make it with the staff wanting to get ready for the arrival of the students. As more staff congregated on the patio, some covering their noses with handkerchiefs, Witaker thought of other ways of getting into the building. But The School was secure, safe from intruders.

Pete Dinato arrived. He joined Witaker on the patio and, together, they tried to think of a way to get into the building. They couldn't. Witaker called the central office but no one had arrived there yet. He was on his own with a major problem.

The first six buses arrived and before he could stop them from unloading, they let about 300 students out and they gathered on the patio with the staff. The 400 people just stood quietly awaiting access to the building. Witaker was just one of them. He had no control over the circumstances.

Witaker called the bus company and told him of the situation and asked them to hold the students on the buses upon arrival at the school. That, however, would create problems for the bus company. It would cause a delay in picking up all the district students because the other schools opened later than the high school

The wet, bedraggled students and staff heard the opening bell ring as they mingled on the patio. The pig manure smell had gotten worse as the westerly winds increased in speed.

A few minutes after the opening bell rang; a face appeared in the office window.

The alarm system had cleared at 7 AM, so it was no longer a problem. But, getting into the building was. The face had a confused look and took in all the people gathered outside. It disappeared for a moment.

Witaker watched as the hallway lights went on and then the main entrance lights.

The figure appeared at the front door and opened it from the inside. Witaker was the first to enter and recognized Homeless Joe. Homeless Joe's odor was perfume to Witaker and the waiting staff and students as the moved into the dry building. Homeless Joe had slept in the building overnight and was awakened by the bell. When he heard no activity, he came to look and quickly analyzed the problem. He had solved Witaker's problem for him.

Everyone now seemed to be in place as the second bell rang. Witaker's master key had access to every room except the entrances. That would be solved later in the day.

Homeless Joe quietly moved away toward wherever his hidden sleeping place was. Witker didn't want to know. The man deserved to be left alone.

Witaker opened his office door and turned on the lights. With the terrible outside conditions when the students were leaving for school, he had made a decision to suspend the dress policy for the day. Just getting everyone into the school was good enough for him.

The first two periods were dedicated to passing out student schedules in a quasi homeroom. During this time Witaker began wrote a touching announcement of the loss of former student, Harry Pearson, the Marine who had given the ultimate sacrifice.

As he wrote the announcement, shafts of sunlight broke through the clouds, shining through his window and illuminating his words. The spirit of Private Harry Pearson rode on the sunbeams and filled the office as he wrote.

At the end of the second period Witaker took the microphone from the communications control panel and began his welcoming comments. He announced the delay in implementing the new dress code and reminded all that it would be in affect tomorrow.

He finished with the announcement of the loss of former student Harry Pearson, the young Marine who had given his life for his country.

On the intercom Witaker said, "Many of you knew Harry Pearson as a friend, a football player, or as a student. In some way he touched us and is a reminder that life is far too short for so many. Please stand as we give a moment to silently show our respect for our lost friend and former student."

From the music room, Mr. Phillips raised his trumpet and played Taps. Through the open music room doors, the sad notes echoed throughout the quietude of the building. The haunting trumpet notes ended and the silence in The School was broken only by the sobs of Homeless Joe from his hiding place somewhere in the building.

The School was in mourning.

Chapter Twenty-Two

A school has been described as four walls with learning inside. Within those walls also are real people with just about every strength and weakness found in the human element. Be they young people or older people, their one common denominator is Their School.

Students will pass through. Staff will retire or leave for other reasons. All are just part of the transience of the inhabitants of the building. Within it friendships are formed, first loves occur, romances wax and wane, careers are made and broken, dreams develop or are dashed. Despite fortunes or failures, all will develop memories of Their School.

For some students, the days in Their School will be their glory days. For others the days will be ones of frustration and angst. Either way, they will remember having been there.

Students become pictures in yearbooks stacked on the shelves in a guidance office. Their pictures indicate the fashions and hairstyles of the days they were there. Their own copies of their yearbooks are stored somewhere in their abodes and moved with them as they relocate to somewhere else. Dusted off before class reunions, the yearbooks are both treasures and remembrances of the days they were in The School.

The School awaits the next edition of the yearbook as the new school year begins.

Whether it was JD Wilson or Brian Witaker at the helm, The School becomes vibrant as bells ring and people move within it. Though the décor may change via paint, bulletin boards or new inside and outside adornments, The School was ready for memories to be made. Its shiny waxed floors will receive the footsteps of an excited population. All will somehow remember the opening day at Their School.

From time to time after leaving, they pass by the structure and recollections flood their minds. From the discussions at Larry's Sports Bar to the chatter at the 20th reunion, everyone has an opinion of the place.

The School is more than just a structure. It is teaching and learning to current occupants and a memory warehouse for those who have left. It is a factory where students enter the receiving door, teachers then stir their creative juices and students depart more knowledgeable through the delivery ceremonies of graduation. The factory has no waste materials, every single student has learned something. Every soul has been touched in some way by being there.

Brian Witaker knew all of this. He had taken his high school yearbook from a shelf at home last night. His mission was to create the happiness he remembered from his high school days for the students coming in the next day. He wanted to be more than the first picture in their yearbook. He wanted to be the unknown reason for their glory days.

Witaker left his office as the third bell rang. He wanted to find the new freshman boy with the parrot colored hair to welcome him to The School.

Chapter Twenty-Three

Brian Witaker exited the office area between the third and fourth periods. The orderly passing of students was quicker than usual as they rushed to find their new lockers. Students greeted him and he returned the greetings with a smile and comments to those he remembered from last year. Witaker realized how important it was to the students to be known by the principal on a first name basis.

As he passed the guidance area, few students seemed to heading into it. They technology of scheduling seemed to have created few conflicts. He did, however, see two young ladies crying as they entered. They were sobbing as they talked about their mutual friend, Harry Pearson. The guidance staff would handle their grief in a professional manner and continue to see others during the day. The overall climate of The School was subdued, a friend had been lost.

Witaker quickly got to the freshman area. He greeted the wide-eyed youngsters who he had met at orientation. He smiled at each of them, patted a few on the back, giving each a "Welcome." All politely responded to his friendly greeting

Alone in the background he saw the boy with the parrot colored hair. Small in stature and wearing torn pants, the boy nervously fiddled with his book bag. He started to turn away as

Witaker approached him. The frightened lad stopped when Witaker called his name.

"Brian Williams!" Witaker exclaimed. "You and I have the same first name and the same initials. I need someone from your class to help me, someone to filter a few ideas I have for the Freshmen and since we have something in common, you would be perfect! Can you help me? And if you can, I can use you right now. You have a study period and I have some extra time."

The nearby students saw and heard the whole thing. They watched as the outcast boy's frightened face beamed at being recognized and being asked for assistance. Brian Williams smiled at Brian Witaker and said, "Sure, Mr. Witaker, I'd like that."

The freshman with the parrot colored hair and The School principal walked through the mass of students hurrying to their next class not unnoticed by the adults and youngsters in the hallway.

Developing trust and respect are key ingredients to learning and Brian Witaker had just modeled it for all. He indeed was the good man in the right place.

Chapter Twenty-Four

The bright rays of the early morning sunshine reflected off Brian Witaker's sunglasses as he drove into the Memorial High School parking lot. It was the Friday before Memorial Day and he had much to do.

Ralph, the new head custodian, had opened all the doors so that clean fresh air could ventilate the building. The scent of blossoming flowers around the flagpole in the circle in front of The School greeted Witaker as he parked his car. The flag pole was barren of the stars and stripes. It would be raised later in a formal ceremony.

The bread and milk delivery men gave Witaker a wave as they passed by. Witaker returned the greetings as he noted the freshly mowed grass and spotless pavement of the empty parking area. The maintenance and custodial crews had done an excellent job in making The School as attractive as possible from the outside.

The principal entered, opened the main office and his office door. He turned on his computer, turned off the air-conditioning and opened the windows. He hung his suit jacket on the hanger behind the door and sat at his desk.

Witaker wanted to start getting ready for the busy day, but since he had arrived early enough to do so, he sat back, clasped his hands behind his head and recalled the events and happenings since the school year began.

It had been a good year by most standards. Educationally it had been a success.

The sophomore class had done extremely well on the state tests. The Honor Society had the most members since The School had opened. The Advanced Placement classes were full. The Board of Education had finally agreed to include Chinese as a foreign language elective for next year. Student attendance was up, suspensions were down. Only one student had dropped out. No one had made a severe mistake worthy of an expulsion. Witaker was proud of the administration, staff, and students. He would tell them so today.

There were several staff changes during the year. DWH left to become a cook in a local restaurant. The owner had not asked for a recommendation resulting in a big loss in customers, particularly those who had any connection with The School.

AD, Joe Ritalli, was relieved of his duties by the Board. Without even having to have the superintendent pressure him into resigning, Joe Ritalli made a major mistake in judgment. On the evening of the meeting of the Football Fathers at the Eagles club, he got arrested for driving under the influence after putting his vehicle into Goat Brook.

Ace Rickets, the retired cop from Larry's Sports Bar, witnessed the accident. Ace fired his snub nosed 38 at the AD as Ritalli tried to swim his way to the shore of the swollen brook. Ace's reasoning was that the man was drowning and needed to put out of his misery. The noise of the swiftly running water masked the sound of the gunshots as Ace missed with all six shots, blasting holes into the sinking car. However, someone heard the sounds of the shots and called the police. Ace had left to retrieve his shotgun at home. By the time he got home, Ace forgot all about the incident and went to bed.

The police pulled the drunken AD from the brook and arrested him. When his vehicle was retrieved from the brook, no one could figure out why there were six bullet holes in it. The

Board put the AD on paid suspension and relieved him of his duties. Joe Ritalli left town after his court hearing. He was convinced that "some son of a bitch was trying to kill him and the gunshots caused him to drive into the brook."

The soccer coach, Mr. Santos, was chosen to be the new athletic director after his team won the state championship. Carlos was the leading scorer in the league and was selected for All State. The team accepted him after the coach fixed him up with a well-endowed sophomore girl who spoke his language. She attended every game and her excited jumping was just enough to produce the level of team testosterone the coach sought.

Coach Santos and Mrs. Thiesman had been a problem for Witaker. Their torrid romance ruined the media center record. After school one day they were caught "frolicking" in an alcove behind the bibliography book stacks.

The media director, a minister's wife, was horrified when told of the incident by Sleeping Beauty who stood and watched for a few minutes, interrupting only when she was sure they were about complete their session, so to speak. The director went to Mr. Witaker and requested a brief leave of absence. She muttered, "God damn Catholics" as she left.

The Santos/Thiesman wedding was held just before the February vacation so that the couple could honeymoon in Brazil. Mr. and Mrs. Witaker attended until a drunken Albert Sanchez took the microphone from the band and began to sing. The Jesuit Latin teacher had wanted to perform the wedding mass even though he lacked the credentials.

The female security person left before Christmas. She was too gentle of a soul and refused to take part in a training session in the double arm bar crotch takedown maneuver. She was not replaced.

For the first time in years, there were no staff pregnancies. Witaker figured that it was an older staff and the younger ones were too tired at the end of the day to do anything except sleep.

Brian Witaker occasionally heard from Mr. Wiles. He had attended a rehap center for his illness and had taken a teaching job at a boy's school to avoid any temptations.

Billy Evans had been officially fired in October. He had easily passed all the requirements to become a real estate agent and had set himself up in an office in town.

He currently was in some trouble because a home he sold as "fully furnished" was without much of the furniture when the buyers tried to move in. Evans had a well decorated condo he had gotten on a foreclosure. He had covered the loss of the missing furnishings in the home he sold by calling the police the day before the closing to report a break-in at the property. He called just after the moving truck he had rented left his condo parking lot.

The football team had a losing season. Once the blinders and headset were removed, the timid quarterback got antsy again. Coach DeBishop stayed with the lad all season and the young man gradually got more confidence. Enough so that the team won two of its last thee games. Alfredo Jimonez was the leading scorer. His six field goals and two extra points made Moon Pie proud.

However, the band was magnificent! Their on-field per-formance was without flaws. Sergeant Popham stood at the top of the bleachers so all the band members could see him. They glanced from their music to him and didn't miss a step. They even had picked up 10 new members, just enough to spell BEAVERS. The gunny sergeant went directly to the top of the bleachers at half time and made everyone leave so that he was alone. His yell, "Clear the friggin' area and stand from be-neath!" was the signal for Mr. Phillips to blow his whistle to begin marching. Because the sergeant had the respect of every-one, no one complained about his language. Neither did Brian Witaker.

The basketball team had trouble dribbling on the new floor and had a modest season. A new student from Croatia had ar-rived just in time to make the team for the final five games. He could nail 40 foot shots with 90% accuracy. But he didn't understand English and decided he didn't want to, based on the garlic smell on the Coach Frasciti's breath. It seemed to the young man that English was a smelly language.

Ms. Aphros was overcome with happiness when the doggy shaped cookie jar was found in the science room between the skulls. Mr. Crane, the savvy science teacher, had discovered it during a class discussion on the human head. He knew of Ms. Aphros' dilemma and had seen the doggy shaped cookie jar in the staff lounge filled with cookies. Using the scientific method, he deduced that ashes other than a dog's were enclosed in the jar. One sniff confirmed his theory. Being a caring soul, he opened the jar and sniffed what appeared to be fuel oil mixed with ash. He removed the ashes and placed them into a container. Using the Bunsen burner, he burned off the oil, took a spare finger bone from a skeleton, and broke it into tiny pieces. He put the mixture back into the jar and gave it to his colleague. Witaker reminded her to take her treasure home with her during the summer.

The new outside security rent-a-cop did a decent job thanks to sergeant Popham.

The sergeant saw him from time to time and gave him explicit instructions on how to take better care of his person. Statements such as, "What dog dumped you here? Shine that belt and those shoes. Pull up those floppy socks. When you are in uniform, look like you earned it. Start looking like you have a pair, not like some piss ant punk!"

The Drama Club's performance had filled the auditorium. They creatively enacted a modified version of *Cats*. All went well until one boy got his tail stuck in an open floor electrical socket while prancing across the stage. When the tail got hooked, the boy was stopped short causing him to do be pulled backward and the following felines ran into him. The jumbled group of actors fell on each other and began to pummel the poor boy that had started it all. A quick thinking director lowered the lights and the hooked actor was freed. He left the stage with his buttocks exposed and holding the tail that had been ripped from his costume in his hand to stop the flow of blood from his nose. The audience politely applauded as the play continued. The only laughter and derogatory comments were in Spanish from the area where Albert Sanchez was sitting. The review in the Memorial High newspaper left out that part of the play. The tail-less boy's sister wrote the article.

The culinary arts program again won a state award. The chefs-to-be rocked the reviewing officials from the state department with a totally different presentation. The teacher, Mr. Baker, had been at the opening day luncheon when Hash Brown's cooks did their routine of *Welcome Back Kotter*. With the help of the hip thrusting young music teacher, they had prepared not only their excellent demonstration cuisine but also a dance spectacular.

After standing behind the food they had created and the judges sampling of it, they stepped out in front of the crab salad, etc. and began. Clad in white chef coats and high chef hats, black checked chef pants and blue sneakers, the twelve young chefs danced to the Elvis song, *Blue Suede Shoes*. Mr. Baker had done a great job of researching the judges. Two older women were big Elvis fans. As Mr. Baker pushed on the start button to start the music, the ladies also got to their feet and began the gyrations they had done at a much earlier age. The students easily won the competition. Even the judge who had chipped a piece of his dentures on a shell in the crab salad voted for them.

Brian Witaker's request for a student Marine ROTC program had been granted. Mr. DeWalt was scheduled to retire at the end of the year. His shop space would be an ideal area for the program. With a few modifications it could be converted into both a classroom and a career area. The Board and the ROTC officials had unanimously selected Gunnery Sergeant Popham as an instructor. A well-respected retired Marine major would direct the program. Any language issues would be his problem.

Mr. Wilson, the driver education teacher, was placed on evaluation assistance. While out on the road with a student driver, he fell asleep as the student got onto the interstate. The unknowing student just kept driving until the car ran out of gas. At 7 PM, Brian Witaker had received a phone call from the state police informing him that a tow truck had just taken the vehicle to a local garage. It was 150 miles away from The School. No one was injured, the gas tank was filled and Mr. Wilson drove the car back to The School.

Arriving after 10 PM, two very angry parents and Witaker met them in the parking lot. The young student was in the back asleep, using his backpack for a pillow. After profound apologies from the teacher, the parents and the student left. Witaker took the keys and sent Mr. Wilson home. It was Wilson's last day as the driver education teacher.

The only other teacher with driver education certification was Ms. Justin. She had a spotless driving record, mainly because she only drove to school and church. Her maximum speed over the past ten years had been 45 miles per hour. Ms. Justin took over the driver education program, but the number of student drivers who had received a driver's license was cut in half. She just couldn't get up enough speed to assist more.

Brian Witaker finally heard from Ms.Ledbetter's attorney in October. Sy Ribinowitz, her lawyer, sent a formal letter informing him that he was being sued for mental anguish and wrongful dismissal. Having no choice, Board attorney Wilford T. Whitemore III, Esq. was assigned to the case. III, Esq. quickly determined that Ms. Ledbetter had no case in the dismissal. She had resigned and her letter was on file. However, the mental anguish argument had some validity.

III. Esq. recommended settlement and the case had been settled out of court. She received one year's pay at the rate of a beginning teacher. Her $30,000 was soon $20,000 after Sy Ribinowitz took his cut. The Board had not given credence to her suit and found Brian Witaker harmless in the matter, but agreed to the settlement just to move on to more pressing issues.

Ms. Ledbetter had taken another teaching job at a nearby high school and was tagged as Ms. Bedwetter the first day of school. The tag was just too much for the young lady to endure.

She resigned before the end of the first marking period. It was rumored that she had connected with Sy Ribinowitz in a romantic way. Those knowledgeable figured her best bet was to use him to get her name changed. Sy certainly wasn't going to give her his name. Sy had a reputation of taking advantage of the client-attorney relationships.

Albert Sanchez's sense of humor had gotten him into trouble in the community.

He was having urinary problems and had scheduled an appointment with an urologist.

His first visit found that he had an enlarged prostate. As the doctor probed his back orifice, Sanchez told the doctor that he loved him. His attempt at humor irritated the doctor but he scheduled a follow-up appointment nonetheless.

Walking into the crowded waiting room for his second appointment, Sanchez carried a dozen red roses with a big ribbon saying, "I Love you and your finger, Doc." The smile on his face quickly turned sour as the doctor appeared at the door to bring in the next patient. Upon seeing Sanchez, the roses, and the ribbon the doctor threw him out. No other doctor would now see Mr. Sanchez. The patients in the waiting room included a member of the Women's Club who quickly spread the word on what had occurred. Mr. Sanchez's wife heard the story and was embarrassed to the point where she left him for a short while. He had given her the unaccepted roses, cutting the ribbon so that it just said, "I Love you."

Brian Witaker had heard about the happening. Since it had no effect on The School other than the embarrassment of having Sanchez as an employee, Witaker just had shaken his head and let it go.

Sanchez had found a free clinic and got his prostate rechecked and appropriate medications. He just changed given his name as A. Sanchez so that the prescriptions could be filled in his name. He spoke Spanish during the entire visit and the staff concluded that he was just another illegal getting free service. Witaker did give Albert Sanchez one open period during the day for "pee purposes." The principal was reaching the age where he might have the same problem.

Slice became a huge asset to The School, Brian Witaker, and Coach DeBishop.

Her husband was a member of the Football Fathers. Their son was a starting tackle on the team. When she heard about the meeting at the Eagles club, she put her husband in marital "time out." She liked Mr. Witaker and Coach DeBishop. They were nice to her and respectful in every way.

To those who haven't experienced marital time out, it works this way. All benefits are suspended in every room in the house including the bedroom and kitchen. There is no conversation, just directives. The offender lives in isolation, takes whatever verbal abuse is forthcoming and minds his manners. Meals, if any, are meager. Laundry service is suspended. Used towels, underwear, shirts, socks collect in a pile. It is an extremely successful ploy. Any attempt at retaliation results in tears, a more dramatic ploy.

Slice's husband lasted one week in time out. He had lost five pounds and gave in because he needed clean clothes. Her request to accompany him to the next Football Fathers meeting was an affirmative. He was warned to be on his best behavior or his parole would be revoked.

Slice attended the meeting in mid September. Her appearance was met with many, "Oh no's!" She knew everyone of the wives from the group. When she got done with the group scolding, she demanded a retreat from their pursuit of what she called two fine men. Every single father agreed knowing what could happen to them if their telephone began ringing after the meeting. They all had had a least one time out session and wanted no more. Moon Pie Jimonez just smiled in the back of the room.

Slice never told Mr. Witaker what she had done, but Moon Pie did. She was really surprised when a gift of one day at the local spa appeared on her desk in a blank envelope. Witaker and DeBishop were truly appreciative of her intervention on their behalves.

123

The head of security had gotten himself into trouble. Online he had purchased a Border Patrol uniform. Wearing the fictitious outfit, he had gone to Home Depot early one morning. Walking toward a large group of Hispanic men awaiting work from any contractor, he identified himself as a member of the Border Patrol. When the men scrambled to get away, one of them ran into shopping cart filled with bagged instant concrete. The man fell into a puddle and the concrete bags broke open. By the time the confusion settled, the poor man was a solid block of concrete from the neck to his shoes.

The head of security split the scene, but not before an orange apron employee recognized him. The security man was verbally applauded in the Letters to The Editor columns in area newspapers and held his job.

Homeless Joe disappeared the third week of school. No knew of his whereabouts. It seemed that he just had left town. Somehow Brian Witaker knew he would see him again some day. He missed having his invisible friend around.

Ralph, the new head custodian, was a treasure to the busy principal. Any graffiti that appeared was cleaned that day. The custodial crew respected the man and he acknowledged their support with mutual respect. The School was proudly clean.

The only real problem with the building that arose during the year was related to the swimming pool. During a meet with the league leading team, the observation window below the water level broke. It happened during a distance race. As the window burst, thousands of gallons of water flooded into the observation room. An assistant coach who was in the room observing was hit by the blast of water and flung into the hallway to the locker rooms. He was found in a corner with a Speedo wrapped around his neck, but uninjured.

So much water had drained from the pool that the swimmers completed the race by walking in their lanes. The state record was broken as a result of the conditions, but it was contested by the record holder. But, somehow, the video tape of the event disappeared and the new record remains in tact.

The pool and flooded areas were pumped. Official estimates of damages did not include the loss of a large bag of hemp in the diving judge's locker.

Another occurrence of embarrassment regarding the swimming team was prior to the flooding one. The banners depicting Memorial High School's records hung over the pool. They were suspended on wires placed well above the pool level. Somehow, the electric timing wire got entangled in the banner wires, causing an electrical short in the wire resulting in the banner wire dropping several feet. It happened just as a diver hit the diving board. At the high point of his leap, he got caught in the lowered wire. He hung suspended above the water until the coach cut the wire. The diver made a perfect entry into the water. The diving judge suspected of drug use gave him a "10", calculating the degree of difficulty at the highest level. It was enough to win the diving competition.

The other team protested the event. Somehow, the video tape of the dive was missing.

The gymnastic team had an excellent year. A major issue arose because a boy was part of the girl's team. The team always dressed at home because their practice and competitions were well after school. Like most female gymnasts, the girls were petite so no one suspected that a boy was participating. He was an excellent athlete and won several events, but stayed away from "girly" events such as the balance beam. All knew him as Jody, a name of either gender. It was his real name. Because no one paid much attention to gymnastics, he went undetected until he met disaster on the uneven parallel bars. Halfway through his routine he lost his grip on the high bar, catapulting his crotch into the low bar at a high speed. The team had to forfeit all the matches in which the boy had been involved. The video tape of the incident made the national news.

Aphros' Ashes defeated Brown's Hair Nets in girls' intramural basketball. They demanded that the trophy be designed as a doggy shaped cookie jar before it was placed into the trophy case.

R2D2's robotic team finished second at the state robotics fair. Their solar driven robot worked well in the parking lot. It was programmed to fire a small rocket into the air and had a tape recording notifying anyone near that the rocket was being launched. The loud "Firing Rocket Off!" gave plenty of warning. However, the fair was held in the capitol armory. The solar panel didn't pick up enough light to make the robot work effectively. The judges were offended as the robot's halting announcement came out as "F...ock Off!" The robot arm was raised only half way. launching the rocket into the judge's table. The video camera taping of the entire fair was destroyed by the rocket.

All had been quiet in Larry's Sports Bar. Witaker had heard a few stories, but they had left him and The School alone. It had cost Ace $2500 to replace the TV over the bar. During an episode of Chad and Laura, Ace became angry when Chad's 16 year-old son from his first marriage yelled at Laura. Ace drew his snub nosed 38 and shot the boy because he "was a young punk". Larry couldn't afford to lose him as a customer so he stayed a regular. He didn't know that Ace, like all cops, had a back-up weapon in an ankle holster. Shotsy and Patsy knew of the other gun and each time something that might anger Ace came on the screen, they switched channels. They stopped doing it when Ace said, "If you do that again...!"

Shotsy got a short lived job, just long enough for him to buy a 'Red Sox Suck' shirt. The XXX large shirt barely covered his expanding middle. He now was a two bar stool man with a cheek on each. Because he occupied two stools, he benefited doubly when some unknowing, generous customer said, "Set up the bar!"

The Football Fathers had a fund raising fair during the time of Spring football practice. Coach DeBishop agreed to sit in the "Sink the Coach" chair. He almost drowned as each of the Fathers took turns hitting the bull's eye and sinking him time and time again.

Someone had even attached a hose to the "sink" tank trying to fill it to the top.

The new dress policy had started out as a mess. One of the senior boys came in wearing leather pants with the backside cut out. He was quickly escorted to the locker room and given a pair of gym shorts to wear over the leather pants. Several girls came in wearing Madonna cone-shaped bras over their sweaters. The local tattoo parlor had experienced a significant decline in breast, lower back, and ankle art work from the younger crowd.

The men faculty had a betting pool on which of the female faculty would be the first to "show some skin." Through what everyone suspected was collusion, Bill Desmond won the money. He had convinced Ms. McCann, the Romantic Poetry teacher, that she should model the women of that time period by wearing uplifting breast supports to demonstrate the female costumes of the Keats era. She even wrote it in her lesson plans, which saved her from any reprimands. Her super structure hit her chin. Her breathing was more intense than ever, the support stuff was just too tight. After her lesson, The School had little difficulties with the dress code policy.

Only one school evacuation had occurred in the Fall. Someone had trapped a skunk in a five gallon pail and had quickly placed a lid on top before the skunk let loose its' wetness. No one knew how the person got the five gallon pail into the building. It just looked a container of floor wax so maybe no one challenged its entry. The clever individual had run a wire from the top of the lid to the girl's locker room door in the gym.

When the locker room door closed at the beginning of the first period, the lid came off and the skunk came out. One of the female gym teachers saw the pole cat, let out a scream and the skunk let it loose. The odor triggered the CO alarm and the school evacuated the building from what most thought was a gas attack. The female PE teacher finally got hold of Mr. Witaker and her story and smell convinced him that it was a skunk.

With all the doors open, the skunk made its way outside and disappeared. The security and custodial staffs isolated the smell in the gym area. The fire department arrived with huge fans and ventilated the area. The female students thought the smell was from Sleeping Beauty while the male students put the odor on DWH.

At half time at a boy's basketball game in which Memorial was playing the Newton Huskies, the crowd in the lobby noticed a large huge trophy in the trophy case. It was bright silver. On the top were two Huskies locked together in a canine embrace, one on top and one below. A large print plastic engraving said, "Better than sniffing it. Right Newton?"

A very angry Newton coach was called out to see it the display. The Huskies trounced the Beavers. Witaker called the Newton principal to apologize. He wanted to stop an obvious similar prank reflecting the Memorial High School mascot when they played at the Newton court.

The educational budget had included 500 new seats in the auditorium. The remaining older seats would be replaced next year. In late September the old seats had been taken out, ADA recommendations for handicapped access were implemented, and 500 new seats were installed. By providing handicapped access in the seating area and to the stage, 20 fewer seats were available. The capacity dropped from 1000 to 980.

Pete Dinato, head of maintenance, and Brian Witaker thought the decrease was insignificant and just notified the central office of the decline. They should have notified all the community users of the auditorium.

The Women's Club used the auditorium for their annual fund raising affair. They had booked the Elvis impersonator who had won the Las Vegas competition for a mid November performance and sold out the place, all 1000 tickets.

The predominately older female audience arrived early. There were no reserved seats, just first come, first seated. As the curtain was ready to rise, twenty angry women were left standing.

During *Love Me Tender*, the opening song, chaos erupted. What should have been swooning turned into screams of turmoil. Twenty unseated women attacked twenty seated ones.

The disruption had a domino effect. Over 100 women, some irked by the noise, began a handbag to head attack. By the time security was able to settle the crowd and the ambulances had arrived, the impersonator had left the stage. The event had been cancelled.

The auditorium rear seating area was bloodied. The floor contained several wigs, a Gucci bag, a broken pair of bifocals, and dozens of 45 rpm records of 1950's vintage.

Six local attorneys became active in suits against the Women's Club and The School. Four local attorneys represented the Women's Club against The School and the Elvis impersonator. Two Las Vegas attorneys represented the impersonator against the Women's Club and The School. Wilfred Whitemore, III Esq. had his hands full.

The day after the event, the changed capacity of the auditorium was posted on the entrance doors. It was a "whoops" for the central office. The local newspaper did not report the chaotic event. The owner's wife was the president of the Women's Club.

Patsy, from Larry's Sports Bar, knew all about the auditorium combat. His wife was one of those who had taken a handbag to the head. He wasn't upset; he figured she had deserved it. He secretly applauded whoever had done it. Mrs. Patsy was a rattlesnake mean reminder who gave Patsy post-it notes of things to do every morning. The green post-its were first time notifications. The orange ones were second time reminders. The red ones signaled danger. Patsy was in permanent marital time out. All except Ace knew of Patsy's marital problems. The others didn't tell Ace for fear he would try to put Patsy out of his misery.

When Patsy told the regulars in the bar about the "broad battle," they were hysterical with delight. Even Ace laughed, but stated that he wanted to shoot that punk Elvis. The regulars were so exited about the possibilities of another such fiasco that they sent a letter to Brian Witaker offering their services as security at the next Women's Club event in the auditorium. In between shots and beers, they had decided that Witaker had planned to have the fewer seats knowing it would create problems for the sold out performance. Witaker was one of them, they concluded!

Brian Witaker put the letter in a special file. At some point during the summer he wanted to drop into Larry's to get support for the newly named school mascot, the Cougars. He had heard that they had developed an artistic rendering of a grey haired woman holding hands with a much younger man. The bar patrons' definition of a cougar, an older woman seeking out younger men, wasn't the kind of Cougar the selection committee had intended.

The newly selected mascot created some problems. A community-wide attempt at drawing the mascot had failed. It seemed that no one even researched what a cougar looked like. A bobcat, a tomcat, a panther, a lion, a leopard, and a kitten had been submitted. The committee had decided to hold another contest during the summer.

Larry's group awaited the new process.

Mark Phillips, the band director, calculated that he needed at least 120 band members to spell COUGARS on the football field. More uniforms needed to be purchased and he had plans to have the varsity and junior varsity baseball teams become quasi members of the band for football games. In band uniforms they would carry clarinets with no mouth pieces and march as band members. The teams would be just enough to fill in the letters.

The recruitment met the approval of the baseball coach. However, all of the baseball team wanted band credits for their participation in the marching band. The decision was on hold.

A major purchasing snafu caused The School some difficulties. When the girl's volleyball coach requested new uniforms, rookie AD Santos made a blunder. The AD/soccer coach was right in the middle of the season and didn't give enough time to selecting uniforms. The only volleyball he had seen was women's beach volleyball. Thus, the uniforms selected were sports bra tops and bikini bottoms. He even got them baseball hats because that is what the women wore on

TV. The uniforms were sent back. Not enough time remained for the second new ones to arrive, so the girls played in the old ones.

AD/Coach Santos had enough problems. The mistake in purchasing uniforms came before his marriage to widow Thiesman. Santos had told the guys at his stag party that the only evidence of her grieving the loss of her dearly beloved was her wearing of black under garments.

The husbands in attendance at the stag told their wives. The wives gossiped. The Italian priest at St. Rosita's got the gossip from one of the wives at confession. In one of his Sunday mass homilies, he pointed to the many black clad Italian widows and said, "That is how one dresses to show the grief of losing a loved one. Not in black underwear!" The women blessed themselves and several whispered to each other, "Sluta!"

When the gossip and news of the homily reached Mrs.Thiesman, Coach Santos was placed into premarital time out. His attempt to compensate for his errors by purchasing two sets of red underwear for his future bride only made matters worse.

Through the good efforts of the school psychologist lending her talents as a marriage counselor, the bride-to-be and groom-to-be were reconciled. The psychologist's comments to disregard the comments made in the homily because the priest, like most men was probably a premature ejaculator, fell on deaf ears. The newly reunited couple quickly left the psychologist's office and made their way to the media center where, behind the biography book stacks, they attempted to consummate their reunion.

The priest from St. Rosita's refused to do the nuptial mass. The director of the media center where the attempted consummation occurred to ruin her no frolicking record, alerted her minister husband. She suspected that he might be contacted to do the marriage ceremony and she definitely told him not to do it if contacted.

The minister, who hadn't frolicked in years, was contacted and performed the ceremony just to spite the priest and his wife. His wife couldn't cook and his bedroom recollections had faded to the point where he only remembered the color of the wall paper. He didn't fear marital time out. He welcomed it.

Through all of the in-school and out-of-school episodes relating the staff, Brian Witaker kept calm. He and his wife just laughed and made note of the human frailties that affected no one except the participants.

Mrs. Witaker happily was the hostess for Mrs. Thiesman/Santos' bridal shower. Most of the gossiping wives attended out of respect for Mrs. Witaker. The wives had rationalized their gossiping as just being the bearers of news. Besides, they all thought they looked much trimmer in the black undies their husbands had given them as gifts.

The senior prom had been a huge success. The class advisors had asked Gunnery Sergeant Popham and his wife to assist in being chaperones. No student got disruptive.

His remarks at the opening of the prom set the tone for the evening.

Before the orchestra began the perform, the sergeant took the microphone and said, "All you pretty girls are to keep those pretty dresses on until you get home at 1 AM to see Mommy and Daddy. All you boys are to keep zippered what you think are is a weapon of mass destruction. It ain't, it just is a brainless little devil that once was used to wet your pants. You boys be gentlemen. I have no desire to mess up my shined shoes with a boot into your nether regions."

Every couple returned home at or before the sergeant's designated time. The members of the orchestra, Mrs. Popham, and the class advisors just smiled during the sergeant's address to the prom attendees. The orchestra leader made a mental note to contact the sergeant. The sergeant was about to get a part-time job addressing every prom they had scheduled for the year.

The junior prom was much different. The junior class advisors were Albert Sanchez and the gyrating music teacher. It was a train wreck.

The class had chosen a local soft rock band to perform. All went well until intermission. Sanchez had been hitting the flask he carried in the hip pocket of his tuxedo. He shared a few sips with the music man and both wives were quite upset with their increasingly loud behavior.

After a brief meeting with the band during which they changed the songs to be played, Sanchez and the music man took the stage with the band. Sanchez took the microphone and sang off-key in Spanish. The music man gyrated wildly to the beat of the music.

The prom kids began to mirror the two on stage. The overactive dancing resulted in one girl being tossed into the set of drums. A young man did a slide into the table with punch and cookies, splitting his rented trousers and cascading the punch into those sitting behind the table. Without the drums, the band lost all control over the beat of the music. They stopped playing and the prom was over by 10 PM.

The cost to The School was $3000 for replacing the set of drums and professional cleaning of the dance floor.

Brian Witaker was furious with the two teachers. Because it was a school sponsored event, he gave both severe letters of reprimand which were the least of their problems. Both men were placed into marital time out. Mrs. Sanchez had given such a Spanish verbal lashing of Sanchez at the end of the prom that he knew he had to change his ways. She also took his flask from him and drove over it as they left the parking area.

Brian Witaker smiled as he remembered the events of the past year. He unclasped his hands from behind his head and went to get a cup of freshly brewed coffee. He had to get ready for the Memorial Day ceremonies

Chapter Twenty-Five

At the end of the fourth period, everyone exited the building to gather around the flag pole in the center circle. Set in the middle of the circle stood a table, podium, microphone, and nine chairs. The Memorial Day assembly was to be a solemn one.

As a means of recognizing his work for the year, Witaker had chosen Ralph to raise the flag. Ralph hooked the flag to the lanyard and slowly raised it to full staff, paused and lowered to half staff. He tied off the rope and made his way to the rear of the assembled.

The band had marched to the rear of the gathered students and began the ceremonies by playing the *National Anthem*. The sharply dressed rent-a-cop gave a hand salute as the band played and everyone else placed their hands over their hearts

One woman and five men preceded Mr. Witaker to the circle as Ralph left. The five men were the teachers who had military service. The woman would be announced later.

Brian Witaker approached the podium and microphone. He wondered about the two additional chairs. He was to be the only speaker, no guest were invited. It was a Memorial High School celebration of the day. He glanced at the table and one very important item was missing.

The clean fresh Spring air was refreshing. Witaker looked to the west and noticed the old farmer standing next to his tractor by his fence. Out of respect for the day, the old timer had not spread manure.

Mr. Witaker gave a solemn review of what Memorial Day meant. He introduced his five service buddies as was the tradition. As each was introduced they stood at attention in front of their chairs

Brian Witaker almost began to panic. The missing item was a large part of the ceremony. He paused.

The pause was interrupted as the band began playing the *Marine Corp Hymn*. From the rear of the school two men marched toward the circle in full dress uniforms. One was in Marine blue and one wore Army brown.

The Marine's left hand held one end of the missing item. The Army man's right hand held the other end. Witaker watched in stunned silence as they approached. They bore the plaque that had been taken from the lobby of the main entrance.

The assembled group made a way for them to enter the circle area. Gunnery Sergeant Popham and US Army sergeant Joseph Pearson brought the missing plaque to the podium. They looked up at the flag, snapped to attention, and saluted the colors at half staff. They then took the two empty chairs.

With tears in his eyes, Memorial High School principal Brian Witaker took the plaque, looked at it, turned to the woman and said, "Engraved on this plaque is the name Pvt. Harry Pearson, USMC, killed in action in Iraq, August, 2008. I have asked his mother, Mrs. Joseph Pearson, to attend our ceremony. She has asked not to speak. We have made a smaller plaque for her and I'd like to present it her now."

Mrs. Pearson stood and accepted the plaque. With tears in her eyes, she moved to where the Army man sat. He stood and she hugged him.

Sergeant Popham had known exactly where Homeless Joe was and salvaged him. The Army man was a highly decorated veteran and with the help of the Veteran's Administration, Joseph Pearson had gotten his life together. Today was his return to Middle Town after nine months of re-becoming himself.

Sobbing could be heard as the gathering returned to the building. Sergeant Popham left to march the band back to the music room. The five teachers with military experience walked back into the building trying not to sniffle.

Mary and Joseph Pearson waited to all had left. They thanked Brian Witaker and gave him a hug. Holding hands, they left. Homeless Joe, Joseph Pearson, was homeless no more.

Ralph took the plaque to set it in place in the lobby. He was sad and happy. He was happy to see Homeless Joe and to find out who he was. But he was sad that one of The School's students would never get to see his own name on the plaque that would be visible to every student who entered the building.

Witaker sat, overcome with his emotions. In the distance a tractor started and moved away into the distance. It would always be a Memorial Day for Brian Witaker.

Chapter Twenty-Six

Graduation was perfect. The clean fresh air gave evidence that the old farmer had gained respect for The School after witnessing the Memorial Day ceremonies. Parents and friends sat on chairs arranged on the football field. A large portable stage was erected fronting the home team bleachers. Two tables filled with diplomas were at the side of the podium and microphone. Six chairs were behind the tables.

As the band played *Pomp and Circumstances*, the entire teaching staff adorned in their college gowns, led the senior class clad in blue and white gowns onto the bleachers.

All tassels were in the correct positions and the class marched in and sat in an orderly fashion. It was a day they would always remember.

A breeze fluttered the American flag behind the bleachers as Brian Witaker, the mayor, chairperson of the Board of Education, the class president and class salutatorian walked onto the stage.

Witaker had advised all speakers that a three minute speech would be enough. All stood for the playing of the *National Anthem* and settled into seats.

Witaker's congratulatory remarks and accompanying accolades for the class were met with polite applause. The mayor gave some brief comments along with a few mentions of his successes as a mayor. It was too good of an opportunity for him to pass up. The next election was in October.

Both students spoke well and received standing ovations from their classmates on the bleachers. The time had come for them to get diplomas. All wanted to put the moment on hold. It was their last day in The School.

The Chairperson of the Board of Education gave out the diplomas as each student's name was called. Both the chairperson and Brian Witaker shook each hand, pausing as parents took pictures.

At the end of the ceremonies, Brian Witaker swept his hand toward the again seated young graduates and said, "Ladies and gentlemen, the new alumni of Memorial High School!" Mortar boards filled the air as the joyous class celebrated in the traditional way.

After more handshaking, more posing for pictures, some hugs from graduates, Brian Witaker returned to his office.

Evening was settling into Middle Town as Witaker dropped into his executive swivel chair. He put his feet onto his desk and clasped his hands behind his increasingly graying head.

Staff members stopped by to give him some recognition for a good year and to wish him a happy summer. He was soon by himself.

It indeed was a good year. Now it was time to begin planning for the next one. He would remember every face of every student who had stepped before him that evening. Good principals do that and Brian Witaker was, indeed, a good principal.

Chapter Twenty-Seven

The walls of The School embraced the new occupants as they entered in September to begin a new year So many new faces, so many faces from the past, so many old stories and so many new stories to be written, The School was the stoic catalyst for each of them.

From the playing fields outside to the smallest closet inside its walls, The School was the mother of all. From her beginning to now, she had nurtured nearly 10,000 people and would be available to do so until she crumbled with age. Her grace would never be forgotten by those who tread within.

Printed in the United States
148448LV00003B/31/P